PITUN'S LAST STAND

An Entertainment about the Fall of Russia

Alexander J. Motyl

Amazon KDP

ISBN-13: 9798717826198
ISBN-10: 1477123456

Cover design by: Art Painter
Library of Congress Control Number: 2018675309
Printed in the United States of America

To Graham Greene and Eric Ambler

Carthago delenda est.

CATO

CONTENTS

UNTITLED

UNTITLED

CHAPTER ONE

Moscow

I still can't decide what was more remarkable—to have seen Russia in ruins or to have met its former master on the Riviera. Both experiences were quite unexpected, at least as far as I was concerned, but not unconnected. The former made the latter possible, though serendipity made it, like so many other things in life and, in particular, in my life, inevitable. The wars that devastated Vladimir Pitun's miserable land also catapulted the tyrant who had in no small measure contributed to that misery into the warm climes of southern France, where his path crossed mine.

But I am running ahead of myself, for the story of my acquaintance with the great Vladimir Vladimirovich Pitun begins not in the lovely city of Nice, and not on its bustling Promenade des Anglais, but in New York, where I live and work for a major newspaper whose name will go unmentioned, but whose reputation is stolid and whose largesse is the envy of poor, unrecognized scribblers the world over. I was supposed to go to Moscow to cover a summit of major oil- and gas-producing nations: the former Soviet Union is my beat and, although my editor never fails to try to flatter me by paying obeisance to my supposed expertise, he also never fails to send me on missions to obscure parts of the globe, on the rationale that anyone who can make sense of the incomprehensible Russians and their incomprehensible soul can make sense of anything. My actual expertise falls far short of such insights, but, since both knowledge and ignorance can be equally great sources of power, I have yet to tell him of his misconceptions.

And then serendipity intervened. Two days before my planned departure for the Russian capital, Pitun, claiming that the human rights of Russian speakers were being violated in northeastern Estonia and invoking a doctrine he had first formulated in his 2014 war against Ukraine, invaded the little country. Naturally, the Russians never used the word invasion. Instead, they insisted they were forced to heed the appeals of a heretofore unknown Russian Democratic Front, which, as the legitimate representative body of Estonia's allegedly downtrodden Russian minority, called on Moscow to rush to its assistance lest their pristine democratic aspirations be crushed by Estonian boots. What else could the democratically-inclined peace-lover *par excellence*, Vladimir Vladimirovich Pitun, do but reluctantly send in the tanks and mobilize the air force?

Forget Moscow, Steve! My crusty editor snarled. Go to Estonia and cover the war. So, I did, especially as I fully expected the escapade to be over in a few days. The Estonian army was minuscule and, notwithstanding its unquestioned heroism and dedication to the homeland, a few thousand Estonians were no match for several hundred thousand well-armed Russian soldiers—I confess that the word horde came all too readily to mind—who, given what I knew about Pitun's love of adventurism (a character trait that I personally ascribed to his diminutive size and the Napoleon complex it engendered), were likely to move from Estonia to Latvia and Lithuania, thereby encircling Belarus and Ukraine and presenting the terrified Europeans and their hapless NATO officials with a *fait accompli*. I figured that the Russians would finish occupying Tallinn airport at just about the time of my arrival. That would make for a great lead sentence, though how I'd continue the story was rather less clear, since it was perfectly possible that the Russians would keep me under lock and key—metaphorically speaking of course: after all, we journalists are a privileged breed—in some godforsaken terminal with nothing but warm beer and stale peanuts for an extended period of time. Something would fall into place; I know enough about the world to know it always does.

When I arrived in Tallinn, to my great surprise the airport was still in Estonian hands. More than that, things were normal. There was no hint of panic, no rumors of impending Russian conquest, no preparations for evacuation. As our Estonian stringer and go-to guy, Andrus, told me on our way to the capital city (his English is probably better than that of most Americans), the reason for the normalcy was shockingly simple—and as unexpected by the Estonians as it was welcome to them. While I was in the air, cramped between two foul-smelling and completely inebriated Finnish businessmen in economy class, what began as a seemingly invincible Russian incursion had morphed into a full-fledged war, but not between Russia and Estonia, as the Russians had hoped, but between Russia and most of her neighbors, as they had not expected. More amazingly still, the neighbors gleefully stabbed the Russians in their back, were now on the offensive, and appeared to be winning.

Apparently, Andrus continued, while exceeding the speed limit in his sleek silver-gray Mercedes and flaunting his superiority by passing every car that dared to dawdle in front of us, Russia's attack on Estonia had served as a signal to all its disgruntled minorities and equally disgruntled neighbors—the former fed up with Moscow's overbearing indifference to their national rights, the latter fed up with Moscow's imperial aspirations—to hit back. Unsurprisingly, the Chechens struck first, taking advantage of the Kremlin's focus on the Baltic to detonate a powerful bomb at the foot of the Kremlin's high walls—at just the place where Soviet and Russian dignitaries are interred —and tearing open a huge hole in the bricks. The damage could easily be repaired—except, of course, for the graves, which were demolished—but the symbolism could not be undone. If the Kremlin was vulnerable, then so, too, was all of Russia. I was surely no less surprised by this daring act than the lugubrious inhabitants of the awful Kremlin.

No less remarkable, considering that all of this took place while I was inhaling alcohol-laden air in a plane, there followed in swift succession a series of assassinations of Russian officials —mayors, governors, military men—in Ingushetia, Dagestan, Bashkortostan, Tatarstan, and Sakha-Yakutia. In the North Caucasus and the Siberian taiga bands of well-armed local guerrillas launched attacks on Russian police and military units, usually inflicting high casualties and mutilating the corpses—presumably as warnings to the civilian Russian population. Andrus, who knew these things far better than I did, suggested that the attacks must have been planned and coordinated well in advance of their actual execution. Yes, I agreed, these minorities must have spent months acquiring weapons and strategizing, while waiting for an appropriate time to strike. It was no wonder that Pitun's hordes had stopped well short of the gates of Tallinn. He had a crisis of major proportions to deal with, in comparison to which Estonia was small fry.

The story, the *real* story, was now in Moscow. I decided to stay in Tallinn for a day or two and produce one by-line to keep my editor happy. Then I'd have to make my way to the Russian capital. The planes and trains weren't running reliably, so that meant going by car. Always on the look-out for freelance work that paid dollars, the entrepreneurial Andrus—whose portly, bald, and middle-aged appearance belied the energy and dedication to his craft that he had manifested during every one of my junkets to the former USSR—volunteered his vehicle and his services and, after placing a ten-gallon container of gas in the trunk and stocking up on sandwiches, soda, and energy bars, we set off at midnight.

When my eyes first alighted on the battered old Zaporozhets, the erstwhile pride of the Soviet automobile industry that would convey us to Moscow, I expressed disappointment and surprise that we wouldn't be taking his Mercedes. "Will this heap make it there and back?" I wondered aloud. But Andrus reassured me that appearances could be deceptive. The motor had been refitted and the jalopy—he actually used that word—would not only make it, but also refrain from tempting car thieves—in contrast to the shiny new Mercedes.

"Believe me, Steven," he said, "it'd be gone in a day and we'd have to walk back."

Andrus knew the backroads and, a few hours after leaving Tallinn, we approached a border crossing south of Lake Pskov—he had decided to avoid Narva, which was likely to be heavily guarded by both the invading Russian forces and their local collaborators—manned by two sleepy Russian soldiers in rumpled olive-drab uniforms. Highly unusual, Andrus whispered. The crossing is never so poorly guarded. They must, he surmised, have been withdrawn to other parts of the country. Is that a good sign? I asked naively. He nodded, though his broad grin betrayed the elation he was feeling. Estonians, I didn't have to remind myself, did not suffer from a surfeit of affection for their elder Russian brother.

One of the guards, a pimply boy with red cheeks, thick glasses, and absurdly magnified bright blue eyes, demanded to see our papers. I showed him my press pass—a fake one that identified me as a correspondent for the Moscow-funded RTV television station—and, evidently ignorant of the concept of a *non sequitur*, he wanted to know what the purpose of our visit was. I pointed to the pass, told him (in good Russian, no less) I was a correspondent for RTV, and, upon seeing that he received this information with a quizzical look on his flat face, explained that we were pro-Russian and funded by Russia and that I had to get to Moscow as soon as possible to tell the world the truth about what was transpiring in Mother Russia. His pal, who stank of moonshine, *samogon*, nudged him with his elbow and grunted, "*Ne pizdi, Seryozha. Ya ustal i khochu vypit.*" Having been instructed not to fuck around because his comrade was tired and wanted a drink, pimply-faced Seryozha stamped our passports, smiled uneasily, and waved us through with "*Vse khorosho*, all is well, *vse khorosho.*"

The roads were surprisingly deserted—oddly enough, most of the traffic was going westward, the importance of which fact I came to appreciate only later—and some ten hours later we arrived in Moscow. I proposed we take lodgings in a cheap hotel on the main drag, the Arbat—I knew the owner, a swarthy Armenian who fit the stereotype of swarthy Armenians, from previous visits and appreciated the unpretentious and clean rooms and the goat cheese, olives, and flat bread served at breakfast—but Andrus shrugged his shoulders and said he had a better idea—the oversized apartment of a friend of his, one Igor Ivanovich Potapov, located in one of the back streets of the centrally placed Kitaigorod district. Potapov, Andrus assured me, was utterly reliable and, better still, he was a great enemy of the regime. He would keep his mouth shut and, being a native of the city and a former secret police officer, would be able to direct us to places that were otherwise inaccessible and to meet people who would not normally be inclined to talk to dastardly *inostrantsy*, or foreigners, like us. Besides, we had no choice but to go to Potapov's, as Andrus had called him from Tallinn and arranged for our stay. You'll see, he said, we'll be quite comfortable. Do you still remember how to drink Russian style? He added slyly.

*

Potapov's flat, as the thick-necked, muscular Russian called it in his serviceable English, was a dilapidated affair that had seen few dusters and mops since his wife died over twenty years ago. Judging from a framed photograph that stood on a sagging bookshelf, I decided that Potapova must have been a formidable woman—big-chested, hair drawn back in a tight bun, a scowl masquerading as a smile on her elongated face. Definitely no Miss Havisham, which may have explained why Potapov did not appear to be touched by even a hint of mourning. Instead, he greeted us with a toothless smile—he later removed his dentures from a murky glass next to the liquor cabinet and placed them in his mouth with a resolute pop—and a bottle of cold vodka. The table was set for three, a basket of thickly cut rye bread stood in the middle, surrounded by small plates of sliced raw onions, cucumbers, marinated tomatoes, grayish sardines swimming in some oily yellow substance, and a C-shaped sausage with enormous chunks of fat just visible below the surface of the casing. Several bottles of beer and Fanta completed the ensemble. It felt like the Soviet Union again.

We took our seats, Potapov poured the vodka into stained tea glasses, cried *"na zdorovye!"*, and, after emitting a groan that hovered somewhere between delight and ecstasy, took a bite of onion, poured himself a beer chaser, and bellowed, "Velcome to Russia!" He downed the beer and wiped his mustache—a brush-like accoutrement that covered his upper lip and, taken together with his soulful eyes, gave him the appearance of a tired walrus—and looking first at me and then at Andrus and then again at me, said, "So, comrades, how can I be helping you?"

"For starters," I replied, "what the hell is going on here? First, there's the Estonian business. And now—assassinations, ambushes." Andrus and Potapov watched as I poured myself a Fanta and bit into a cucumber. "I mean, who's in charge? And why the hell isn't Pitun doing anything about it? He's president, after all." The questions, I realized too late, were naïve and would hardly inspire Potapov's confidence in my abilities.

Potapov reciprocated with a crooked smile, as if he were an exasperated school teacher dealing with the class dunce. He filled our glasses, proposed that we drink to peace and understanding, and sat back. While I wondered whether his invocation of Soviet toasts was a stab at irony on his part or a mark of nostalgia for the good old days, he broke off a piece of sausage, shoved it into his mouth with a satisfied grunt, and, his eyes glistening with alcoholic cheer, pointed a greasy finger at me.

"He funny guy, Andrus! He one funny guy." Suspecting that an explanation delivered in broken English would be too much for my impatient ears, I repeated my questions in Russian and hoped he would take the hint and reply likewise. He did.

"You must understand," he began, "that the great Pitun is not so great. You Western journalists and so-called experts think of him as a masterful chess player." He turned to Andrus. "Don't you always say that, while Pitun is playing chess, you are playing checkers?" Potapov sniggered sardonically, as Andrus nodded. "You are wrong, my friends, so very, very wrong." Potapov was staring at me now. "Pitun is an amateur, a little boy in shorts. He happened to be in the right place at the right time. You remember the 1990s? Russia was collapsing. Our president was a drunk. And Pitun mounts a big white stallion and rides into the city promising law and order and greatness at precisely the time that—"

"Energy prices went through the roof," I interjected, hoping to redeem my battered image as an expert.

"Exactly!" cried Potapov. "*Tochno!* We Russians wanted a tsar and Pitun gave us a tsar." Potapov stroked his mustache and looked around the room distractedly before breaking off another piece of sausage. I watched two bits of fat bounce off his plate and fall to the floor. "And he gave them one more thing— a feeling of greatness. Don't look so surprised, my dear Andrusha. We Russians need to believe we are great. It doesn't matter whether we are. After all, the country is a toilet and everyone knows that, but"—Potapov carefully placed a slice of sausage on a piece of bread and pushed the contraption into his mouth —"we must believe that there is no other toilet like ours in the world."

Potapov swung his arms majestically in a great arc. He lowered them like a dying swan in Tchaikovsky's ballet and concluded with operatic finality: "Pitun has been lucky. His luck ran out years ago, but you Americans were too stupid to see that. And now," he looked me straight in the eyes, while I resisted the temptation to run away, "and now Pitun is paying the price for his stupidity and negligence, especially during the corona virus crisis. We survived that—barely, with no thanks to the great Pitun." Potapov's eyebrows rose, creasing his aged forehead and creating the impression that he was speaking of something that concerned him not a whit, and he shrugged. "And now it is the end—*konets*."

"For Pitun?"

"Obviously, but he no longer matters." His eyes appeared to well up with tears. "My friends, it is the end of Russia." Potapov lay both hands on the table and leaned forward, his wet lips quivering. "This is just the beginning—these assassinations, these attacks. Soon, very soon, maybe even tomorrow, there will be war. We have made everyone hate us and now we will have to pay the price." He wiped his eyes and reached for the bottle. "There is no escaping fate, my friends. Are you fatalists? Perhaps we should all be. But, first, let us drink. What else is there to do when your world, your home, your life is about to collapse?"

I suspected that Potapov was, in typically melodramatic Russian fashion, overstating the case, but, my tongue tied by his pessimism and my head blurry from the alcohol and lack of sleep, I said nothing. Andrus, who could have justifiably been expected to give in to temptation and gloat, also remained silent.

*

The next day proved me wrong. With Moscow's attention diverted to Estonia and its rebellious provinces, Ukraine launched a full-scale offensive against the depleted Russian forces stationed in the Crimea and along Russia's border with the secessionist bits of the Donbas. The assassinations and guerrilla attacks, meanwhile, picked up steam and scores more took place throughout the North Caucasus, the territories inhabited by the Volga Tatars, and a broad swath of Siberia and the Far East. Mutilations—severed noses, tongues, and, occasionally, genitalia—now appeared to have become the norm throughout much of Russia. Leaflets written in broken Russian were also being distributed, warning local Russians to leave the non-Russian territories or face death. Panicky telephone calls clogged the air waves as the inhabitants of Saint Petersburg and Moscow frantically sought news of their friends and relatives scattered throughout the vast Russian Federation. Social media were rife with rumors of marauding, murderous "slant-eyes", bloodthirsty fascists, nationalist cutthroats, genocidal maniacs, and other riff-raff out to kill innocent Russians.

I had no doubt that the growing chaos in Russia's provinces was bringing out the worst in the lumpen, but, Potapov's views still ringing in my ears, I was absolutely certain that most of the attacks, though horrible to contemplate, were acts of vengeance for perceived and real wrongs committed by Pitun and his supporters, who, alas, were legion. For, despite all his faults, despite his being a poor chess player and fool who hadn't understood that he should have stepped down years ago, the people—the simple *narod* beloved of Russia's deluded nineteenth-century poets and writers—admired and adored the man. It was the intelligentsia that despised him, although even they included not a few mercenaries willing to sacrifice their ideals and their calling for thirty pieces of silver. Pitun knew how to keep his people in line. He gave them bread, he gave them circuses in the form of his own macho antics, and he gave them a sense of pride in their own benighted selves. As Potapov said, Russia was—or had become—a toilet, but it was supposedly the best toilet in the world.

Unfortunately, Pitun had also deprived the Russians of any claim to innocence. And it was no surprise that many non-Russians interpreted the absence of innocence as the presence of guilt—for the crimes against humanity that Pitun had committed and that the Russians had countenanced if not actively approved. There was no such thing as collective guilt. I knew that. But I also knew that, if there were, it would apply wholeheartedly to the Russians Pitun had created. Spineless, drunk with greatness, and fanatically committed to a mad tyrant, they bore much of the moral responsibility for his actions. They were hated and now they were paying for the hatred they had expressed and engendered.

My ruminations, which had been taking place as I drank some black tea and chewed on a piece of stale bread, were interrupted by a tremendous explosion. The three of us ran to the window and saw several delicate plumes of smoke rising from the direction of the Kremlin. I slipped into my jacket, ascertained that I had my pad and pen, grabbed my camera, ran my fingers through my hair, and, accompanied by the equally disheveled Andrus, dashed through the door without saying adieu and bounded down the creaking stairs. The whole building was in uproar, as a crowd of gesticulating and chattering Russians gathered outside. *"Eto navernoe Kreml,"* an unshaven man in soiled pajamas said. "It's probably the Kremlin."

Andrus and I followed the streaming crowd and ran toward Red Square. Sirens blared, ambulances zigzagged among the cars and pedestrians, policemen and soldiers, their rifles in their hands and their guns cocked, rushed ahead, their exact destination unknown. As we reached the square, I realized that Potapov's neighbor had been wrong. The explosion hadn't rocked the Kremlin's high walls again. That, presumably, would have been overkill, according to the Chechen masterminds behind the deed. Instead, the blast had destroyed one side of Saint Basil's, the magnificent cathedral with the fabulous multi-colored onion domes. We stopped, shocked by what we were witnessing, and, as I readied my camera, we watched with horror as the rest of the edifice began crumbling in slow motion, almost as if we were watching an old film, and, within a few seconds, perhaps no more than ten, the whole pile of bricks and icons came crashing down, sending up a colossal cloud of thick, pungent dust.

The crowd stopped moving, as everyone was transfixed

by the unfolding tragedy. When the crash finally came, a deep groan emerged from the depths of their guts and took flight, like a flock of crows. The dust slowly lifted, revealing a massive mound of debris among which lay curved parts of the domes and gleaming remnants of golden crosses. Hundreds of years of Russian culture had vanished in an instant. And then, frantically, the crossings and mumblings of prayers began, followed by the wailing, the tears, the kneeling, and waving of arms. How could one not pity so pathetic a people? They may have supported and behaved like criminals, they may have willfully danced on the graves of foreign cultures, but even criminals, even mass murderers can elicit pity when reduced to such desperate straits.

I had no time to pursue that line of thought, however, as almost immediately after the cathedral had imploded, two more explosions shook Red Square. Lenin's Mausoleum, so long the central adornment of the huge space that featured annual displays of Russia's military might, seemed to rise into the air and then, as pieces of black marble flew in all directions, settled into a smoking heap, with which whatever remained of Lenin's mummified body was presumably commingled. A fitting end, I thought, to the mass murderer who destroyed Old Russia and replaced it with a monstrous experiment in human engineering that had killed millions and made Stalin inevitable.

The second explosion—or was it several simultaneous explosions? I couldn't tell—took place to our right. The delicate towers of the beautiful old GUM department store fell silently, while the vaulted glass roof exploded into millions of shards and rained down on the helpless masses below. The crowds, which had rushed toward the GUM in order to escape the destruction of the cathedral and the mausoleum, now reversed course and ran back to the center of the square. Colliding and falling bodies, screams and yells, and curses and prayers completed the picture of complete mayhem.

I had no doubt that all four explosions were the work of

the Chechens. As I surveyed Red Square, I decided there would probably be no fifth, at least not here. The major architectural landmarks had been attacked or destroyed. The point had been made; the message was clear. Chechnya had declared war against Russia and, this time, the war would be fought entirely on Russian, and not Chechen, lands.

As we pivoted toward the Kremlin gates, a wail went through the crowd: "*Pitun, spasi nas! Spasi nas! Spasi nas!*" Would Pitun answer their entreaties and save them? I wondered. It was high time for the all-powerful dictator to make an appearance, reassure his people that all was well and that all would be well, and undertake some countermeasures. Instead, like Stalin after Hitler's invasion of the Soviet Union in 1941, Pitun appeared to be in hiding. As were his henchmen, the heads of the secret police, internal affairs ministry, and national guard, the top generals, and his key financial backers among the so-called oligarchs. Were they planning a counterattack? Were they plotting to remove Pitun? I shared my suppositions with Andrus and he agreed that something had to be afoot. Russians never just turned over and died.

As it happened, that may have been true of the Russians, but not of Vladimir Vladimirovich Pitun and his buddies. For, as we were speculating about what was really going on, Pitun and Co. were, as I learned a few hours later, boarding their private planes and fleeing the country—presumably to their luxurious villas in such sunny safe havens as the Caymans, Cyprus, Monaco, and Palm Beach.

*

Once the world had learned of Pitun's flight, all hell broke loose in and around Russia. There were reports of non-Russians —especially Ukrainians, Crimean Tatars, Bashkirs, Chechens, and Estonians—dancing in the streets, throwing offal and excrement at Russian embassies and consulates, defacing Russian-language signs, and tearing down Soviet war monuments to unknown soldiers and victorious liberators. Knowing how deeply the non-Russians resented their former and sometimes current colonizers, I did not doubt the veracity of the reports. Pitun had ruled with violence and it was no surprise that his demise was also greeted with violence.

More important was that his departure suddenly created a power vacuum within the very heart of the Russian polity. For the first time in decades, this vast land was without a ruler. I knew from Russian history that, when such circumstances prevailed, chaos inevitably ensued, as various factions struggled for power, private citizens took the law into their own hands and pillaged to their hearts' content, minorities took advantage of the confusion to advance their own claims, and outside powers (such as the Poles during the Time of Troubles in the late sixteenth and early seventeenth centuries) launched attacks and hoped to bite off chunks of Mother Russia's voluminous body. The Ukrainians had already struck. Who would be next?

I got my answer next day. The Kazakh army drove its top-shelf tanks and Chinese-built armored personnel carriers into the vast steppes of northern Kazakhstan and gave the resident Russian population exactly twenty-four hours in which to pack their essentials and make haste for the *Rodina*-Homeland. The Georgians shelled Russian positions in Abkhazia and South Ossetia and managed to drive the occupying forces out. The Moldovans gave the government of the Transnistrian Republic two hours to surrender or to suffer invasion, capture, and execution. The Transnistrians immediately capitulated: their armed forces were larger than Moldova's, but they obviously sensed that the gig was up and that resistance would be futile.

"Watch us and the Latvians," Andrus said. "We'll be next."

He was right. Two days later, Estonian and Latvian radicals—the Russian press called them extremist fascists— launched brutal attacks on anyone unwilling or unable to speak their native languages. A mass exodus of Russians began, driven more by fear of what might happen than by the reality of what had happened, with thousands going eastwards and just as many crossing into Kaliningrad province and hoping to make it to Germany via Poland. Unsurprisingly, the Poles dispatched several battalions to their border, which they reinforced with barbed wire and ditches. The Germans, meanwhile, called on everyone to engage in negotiations and abjure violence; the French regretted that so many attributes of world civilization were being demolished; the European Union expressed its deepest concern and hoped for a peaceful resolution; the Americans wondered who was minding the nuclear arsenal.

What shocked me most was that Minsk also got on the bandwagon. The supine Belarusian regime, renowned for never saying *nyet* to its Russian masters, no matter how gross their provocations and how offensive their arrogance, finally got the courage to say no. The Belarusian president called for a total mobilization of the armed forces and, once the units were in place, gently suggested to the Russian officials stationed in his country that they were most welcome to leave at their earliest convenience as he could not, alas, guarantee their security in light of the growing popular anger.

Where was, I wondered over supper at Potapov's, the Russian army? With over a million men in uniform and armed with all the latest weapons and electronic gadgets, it had been the pride of Pitun's regime, the symbol of the greatness that he was bestowing upon the deservedly proud Russian nation. Granted, they were leaderless, but, even so, their love of country should have compensated for that and led some of them to put up a fight. Instead, they appeared to have melted away—as in 1916 and 1917, when thousands of Russian soldiers deserted from the German front and returned to their villages with empty guts and loaded rifles and helped their compatriots pillage, rape, and burn. That was, I knew, the beginning of the revolution that toppled the Tsar and enabled Lenin's band of Bolsheviks to seize power. Would there be another revolution today?

"You have," Potapov replied, "answered your own question. They have gone, melted away, disappeared—poof!" The fingers of both his powerful hands sprang wide open to make the point. (How many throats, I inadvertently thought, had they squeezed?) "These stupid, poor Russian boys were never Pitun's. He thought he had them by the balls, but he didn't. They are simpletons, good, honest Russians, so they remained true to their villages, their towns, their neighborhoods." His fingers closed sharply and formed two fists. "There is trouble, there is chaos, and what do they do? They run home, of course! My friends, the Russian army is dead! And that means the regime is dead. Pitun thought he would rule for a thousand years. Instead, the coward and thief has run away and, like all tsars, has left a mess for his people."

"But you'll manage," I said encouragingly, without specifying whether I meant Potapov or the Russians, "won't you?"

Potapov shook his head sadly. "This time, *nyet*."

*

Potapov was well into his seventies, although, given the Russian propensity for premature aging, he could just as well have been in his fifties. But I knew he had served in the Committee for State Security, the KGB, in Soviet times, which meant that the higher age estimate was far more likely than the lower one. Andrus had said little about just what Potapov did in the KGB, but his tenure certainly didn't testify to his high moral qualities, at least by the standards of the civilized world. Pitun had also been a KGB officer, though a minor one stationed someplace in East Germany, and his choice of career went a long way to explaining his preference for sticks to carrots. But Pitun looked vicious; he looked like a killer, even though he probably never shot anyone in his life. He was known to love to hunt—photographs of him with a Siberian tiger he bagged had made the news some time ago—and he ordered many an assassination (London, which drew his exiled political opponents, appeared to be a favorite site for Russian "wet work"), but, like most tyrants, he was too much of a coward to pull a trigger himself and watch crania explode.

As to Potapov, who knew? He looked avuncular thanks to his large drooping eyes and bushy mustache. The slowness and deliberateness of his movements also seemed to suggest that he was probably an analyst, and not a field agent who had to count on swift reflexes and adrenalin rushes. Of course, that was all in the past and I was enough of an old Russia hand to live and let live and to ignore people's backgrounds. Too fastidious an insistence on impeccably clean hands would have translated into complete isolation, for the sad fact about contemporary Russia was that no one, absolutely no one, was innocent. If they hadn't collaborated, supported, tolerated or benefited from Communist rule, then they collaborated, supported, tolerated or benefited from post-Communist rule. There was no escape. Everybody was tainted and everybody was guilty, at least to some degree. I had learned to put aside my naively American moral standards—ones that we were more than willing to violate whenever convenient—and think in Asian, or more exactly in Eurasian, terms when I visited Russia or any of the post-Soviet states.

All of us were visibly exhausted, Andrus and I from witnessing the carnage on Red Square, Potapov from the emotional turmoil of watching his country self-destroy, but I resolved to ask our Russian guest a few more questions. Who knew what tomorrow would bring and whether I'd have another opportunity to interrogate him?

"It must," I declared, "be especially hard for you." His eyebrows shot up quizzically. "I mean, having defended Russia all your life, having devoted so much of yourself to your country, and now"—this time, it was my turn to move my hands, slowly and dramatically, in a broad arc—"to watch it collapse before your very eyes." I brought my hands together swiftly in a loud clap and both Andrus and Potapov jerked back in their chairs. I felt I needed to say something to complete the performance, so I concluded, weakly alas, with a question that the Russian had already answered: "Is it really the end?"

Fortunately, he was too tired or too depressed to respond in schoolmarmish fashion. "*Konets*," he announced definitively, "the end." His lips were quivering and his hands (which had, again I thought, squeezed throats or written analyses or pulled triggers) were shaking. The good Andrus cast a glance at me and produced a barely perceptible nod in Potapov's direction. He was imploring me to stop, but I couldn't, of course, or, rather, I wouldn't. I had a story to write. I needed information. And Potapov was a fantastic source that I could not, would not, slip out of my hands, no matter how overcome with physical and moral fatigue he may have been.

"But the security services, the generals," I continued, "surely they'll organize and fight back. Even in 1918 and 1919, the old regime defended itself and, for a while, it looked like the Whites could even win. Denikin almost made it to Moscow, didn't he?"

He waved his hand dismissively, as if chasing away some bothersome fly. "Those were different times. Then, the old regime still believed in itself. As did the Bolsheviks. It was a clash of two beliefs and two forces who were being challenged —by history, of course—to demonstrate just how much violence they were willing to employ to promote their ideas. The Bolsheviks were stronger, more ruthless. So, they won." He was breathing rapidly, evidently moved by the tragic drama of his nation's history. "But today," Potapov pursed his lips and inhaled and exhaled several times, "today there are no heroes, no believers anymore. Of course," he waved both hands again, "of course, they will organize. They will fight. They will resist. But they will lose. Who believes in Pitun and the Russia he created? Only idiots and criminals. Who will die for such a monstrosity?" He cleared his throat and spat into a cloth napkin. "No one.

"Naturally, there will be fighting, there will be war. Thousands, maybe millions will die. But," his eyes looked moist again, "they will be mostly Russians." Turning to Andrus, he said, "Pour me a glass, *dorogoi*. I need a drink." And then back to me: "You can't fight the world and expect to win. Pitun was an idiot—a *durak*. He made enemies with everyone—everyone. Can you believe that even the Belarusians—who, even after those mass demonstrations, still have no idea what makes them different from us—hate us? They will all rise up," he announced portentously, his voice assuming prophetic tones, "every one of the nations we oppressed inside the Russian Federation and every nation on our borders. They will rise up and kill us." His eyes focused on mine as his tone became harsh and cynical. "And what will the freedom-loving West do? What will your great country do?"

I knew the answer. "Nothing."

"Exactly," he said with a bizarrely triumphant voice, as if he were the attacker and not the defender. "The world will do nothing. Instead, you will laugh in your sleeves, shed crocodile tears, and wait for the apocalypse to descend on all of my country." He sobbed loudly, and genuinely, slapped his own cheek so as to restore some semblance of reality, and announced, but not before saying he would put me in touch with some excellent sources, that he was going to sleep. "*Ya tak ustal*," he said slowly. "I am so tired." He looked it.

Andrus and I stayed sitting at the kitchen table. Several moths flitted about nervously near a solitary light bulb hanging from a twisted wire. The refrigerator, an old model from several decades ago, hummed erratically. I espied a cockroach scurrying across the face of the olive-green cupboards. Muffled shouts from within the building—an argument? A fight? A drunken man beating his wife? A drunken woman beating her husband? —broke the silence every few seconds. If this was the calm before the storm, then it was a very disquieting calm that portended the storm and did not lull one into complacence.

I turned to Andrus, who was staring at the food on his plate. "The bloodshed aside, you must be delighted by what is happening here. The end of Russia and the triumph of Estonia, no?"

He smiled hesitantly and fidgeted briefly in his chair before replying. "The bloodshed is a tragedy, of course"—I knew a *but* was coming—"but yes, it is true. Russia's collapse is good for us." And then he added, lest I mistake his approbation of ongoing events as *Schadenfreude* (a disposition that many Central and East Europeans share and enjoy, especially with respect to Russia), "And good for the world—very good for the world." After a beat or two, he made another qualification. "That said, we must be careful. There will be war, there will be economic collapse, there will be refugees. Millions. And they will all go to Europe. Did you notice that, while traveling here, all the cars were going in the other direction?" I had, I said, but hadn't made much of it then. "Rats escaping a sinking ship," he averred. "Russians hoping to make it to Estonia, to Latvia—to anywhere, as long as it's not Russia." Andrus emptied the bottle in our glasses and raised his. "To Mother Russia! May she die a peaceful death and never be resurrected." I was unsure of what to say in response, so I chimed in with a "cheers," and drank the tepid liquid. Several hours had passed and the formerly ice-cold vodka had acquired the taste of lukewarm tea—an apt metaphor, perhaps, for the condition of Pitun's regime.

*

We left the house at dawn and made our way for Red Square. Normally, after several such explosions, the affected spaces would be cordoned off and be swarming with police and soldiers. Testifying to the breakdown of authority in the city, Red Square stood unguarded, as if it were telling the Chechens that it was too tired and too indifferent to care about more attacks. Knots of people stood about, talking softly and gesticulating nervously. The smoke and dust from the blasts had disappeared and all we could see now was the façade that hung on the skeletal girders of the GUM, the rubble that used to be Saint Basil's and Lenin's Mausoleum, and the breached wall of the Kremlin. Unwittingly, I thought of the Ottoman capture of Constantinople in 1453, when Sultan Mehmet's Janissaries broke through the invincible walls erected by Constantine the Great and laid waste a Byzantine culture that had dominated that part of the world for over a thousand years. That was a turning point in history. So, too, was this.

"Let's go to the Kremlin," I proffered. "Believe it or not, but I've actually never been inside."

"The guards won't let us in," Andrus objected.

"Perhaps there aren't any? If Potapov is right, we may be able to walk right in."

Which is exactly what we did. The gates were open, the police were absent, and mobs of young men and women were busy ransacking the buildings and appropriating, in the time-honored fashion of Russian peasant rebellions, whatever they could lay their hands on. Papers, documents, newspapers swirled in the gusts of wind that swept through the insides of the fortress. Here and there, fully ignored, lay bloodied corpses, sometimes of soldiers, mostly of civilians. Yells, shouts, screams resounded in the alcohol-laden air. The mobs were drunk, of course, and felt fully emboldened—nay, entitled—to take what had been taken from them in the course of several hundred years. Russians were traditionally respectful of and subservient to authority, except when they weren't. And when they weren't, as inevitably transpired every few decades, the results were horrific. Likes swarms of locusts, like Mongol hordes, they swept across a city, town, or village and destroyed everything in their path. I took a few dozen photographs—for some, the revelers even posed with their trophies in their hands—and then, saddened and depressed by the carnival-like Jacquerie, I grabbed Andrus's arm and led him toward the exit. Needing no prodding, he followed willingly.

Red Square had attracted many more curious onlookers and some scattered policemen and soldiers. The latter were milling about the bomb sites, uncertain about what exactly they were to do. We approached a small group of Russian men heatedly debating something. One cursed Pitun and shook his fist at the unresponsive heavens. Another spat on the ground and wished the Chechens to go to hell. Still another damned the Ukrainian and Estonian fascists for their betrayal of Russia. "What did we do to deserve such treachery?" he cried, his voice cracking. After tempers settled down, their discussion became serious. "What now?" someone asked. "We will die," someone else answered. "*Nyet, budem borotsya,*" shouted yet another, "we will fight!" That heroic declaration was followed by a cacophony of voices exceeding one another in bravado. "We will fight the world!" "We will eradicate the Chechen plague!" "And the Ukrainians and Estonians and all the other vermin!" After a moment of silence, a timid voice spoke up, "It is time to go home and pack our belongings and run, my friends. There is no alternative..." His voice trailed off. I expected a volley of protests, but, instead, the group soundlessly dispersed.

We wandered over to what remained of Lenin and his mausoleum. The wreckage—variously sized chunks of marble strewn about chaotically—reminded me of an ancient Greek site that had been exposed to searing fires and crushed underfoot by barbarians. Several men and women were poking amid the rubble with canes. I pointed at them and turned quizzically toward Andrus. "Looking for bits of Lenin, I suppose," he answered. As we approached them, I noticed they were all old, the gnarled men in stubby jackets and smudged hats, the pale women in somber kerchiefs and with toothless grins—remnants, like the rubble, of better Soviet days.

"What's that?" I had noticed a light-colored piece of something that glistened in the sun.

Andrus bent over to examine it, straightened his back, placed his hands on my shoulders, and, grinning broadly, informed me that "It looks like a fingernail—probably the great Leader's. Would you like to have it"—he took a few seconds to take note of the ashen look on my face—"as a kind of *memento mori?*"

Shuddering, I drew back in horror. "Let's get out of here, for God's sake," I said hurriedly and set off toward the GUM.

*

The late nineteenth-century structure had been one of my favorite buildings in Moscow and I used to love sauntering along the length of the store and admiring how the seemingly endless curved glass ceiling and supporting tiered walls approached their vanishing point at the far end of the enormous building. The GUM was like Russia, vast and limitless and seemingly eternal. Now, as I surveyed what remained of the store, I concluded that the simile was quite apt. Both store and country had seemed indestructible—until they both fell victim to destruction. Like Andrus, I could shed no tears for Russia; and, like Andrus, I did shed metaphorical tears for the GUM. Countries, empires, and states had a right to come and go; cultures should stick around, preferably forever.

The looters had been here as well. Hundreds were still rummaging about, loaded down with clothes, lamps, jewelry, and other items that had been inaccessible to them in normal times. Groups of men were removing sofas, easy chairs, tables, and desks. Bathed in all manner of perfumes, women carried reams of material and bags full of cosmetics. Children were gorging themselves on sweets. Not to be outdone by the customers, the store personnel had no qualms about taking part in the Bacchanalia. No one paid any attention to the dead and wounded, moaning, mangled bodies strewn about like discarded mannequins. Andrus espied a golden ring at his feet and grabbed it.

"For my wife," he mumbled tersely, visibly embarrassed by his having succumbed to the logic of the mob. "She didn't want me to go with you. Said it would be too dangerous. Made a scene." He dropped it into his pocket. "This'll soothe her temper."

I had seen enough. Russia was collapsing before my eyes. The Chechen bombings, the assassinations and attacks, the ethnic cleansings, and the Ukrainian offensive were elaborations on politics as usual. After all, wasn't it the Prussian von Clausewitz who had written that war was politics by other means? But this—the looting, the brazen, unabashed thievery, the rummaging about for pieces of Lenin (as if he were a saint whose remains could produce miracles!)—was too much. When a people, a nation, a *narod*—whether Russian or not—loses all control of itself and reverts to a Hobbesian state of nature, then it was indeed the end. Once again, as so often in their history, the Russians had proven to be their own worst enemies.

This was dispiriting and I needed to get out of this carnage. "Potapov suggested we see someone at the Bolshoi," I said. "That could be an interesting angle." As we exited the ruins of the once magnificent GUM, I added, "And let's get a drink somewhere. I need a drink. A big drink." Andrus, silent and probably as affected as I was, nodded.

Unfortunately, that drink was not to be and neither was the Bolshoi, for, at precisely the moment that Andrus had finished nodding, a series of discordant ra-ta-tats broke out, punctuating the general murmur that had settled over the square and transforming yells of recognition or discovery into screams. The crowd, which had swelled to many thousands by now—I glanced at my watch and saw that it was noon—transmogrified into a flood of panic-stricken bodies flowing in all directions and sweeping away whatever stood in their path. We pressed our backs to the wall of the department store and, with bated breath and tightened chests, watched the mayhem unfold.

"Chechentsy! Chechentsy!" people cried hysterically, but whether it was in fact the Chechens who had come back to do

some mopping up or whether it was the police or army or, for that matter, entrepreneurial gangsters who wished to have a go at looting no one could tell for sure. They ran. They ran without regard for the people in their way. Women, children, old men tumbled to the ground before our eyes and were trampled underfoot. And we could do nothing, except watch and hope that we would remain unscathed. After taking a few photographs, I hid the camera in my breast pocket and shut my eyes. I opened them only some fifteen or more minutes later, when the stampede had ended and all that remained was a battlefield with the dead and wounded strewn about, with legs and arms and heads crazily arranged at odd angles, and with desperate moans and groans filling the rancid air.

We picked our way among the bloodied, mangled torsos, heads, and limbs and left the charnel house that Red Square had become. "Come, let's go here," Andrus guided me gingerly by my arm into a hole-in-the-wall bar. "We can get a drink here." The place was empty: evidently, the owner and waiters had fled with the crowd without bothering to lock up. Andrus grabbed a bottle of Johnny Walker Black and poured us two large drinks. We downed them immediately and he poured two more. We didn't stop until, six pourings later, the bottle was empty and we felt strong enough and addled enough, once again, to confront the sad reality of Pitun's Russia.

*

Although Red Square was eerily still, the streets surrounding it were bursting with nervous human activity that reminded me of grainy photographs of Russia during the Revolution of 1917. Strolling had ceased, replaced by an accelerated walking or running. Smiles had vanished, even as they had always been a rare commodity in Pitun's capital. Brows were furrowed, heads were bent downward, arms were swung rapidly. Most striking was the relative absence of vehicles—perhaps because those Muscovites with cars had already left the city or because their owners figured they might be assaulted by mobs on the lookout for excess wealth. Hating vacuums, the crowds spilled into the streets and created the impression of a mass demonstration. Except that there were no demonstrations. People had become visibly atomized. They joined groups briefly and then immediately departed, presumably searching for news, hoping for hints of optimism amid the gloom surrounding them like an impenetrable fog. Russians were never known to be individualists, but they were known for turning inward, like monks and ascetics, whenever the world seemed to be ending. And the world around them, at least here in central Moscow, was indeed ending.

That thought led me to suggest to Andrus that we head for the outskirts and measure the pulse of society there. We could, I went on, even leave Moscow. There was nothing more for me to do here. I had seen the death and destruction and, even if things got worse, my story wouldn't change. There were no officials to talk to, as they had all either fled or were in hiding. Potapov's contact in the Bolshoi might be interesting, but I could easily forego a disquisition on the state of Russian opera and ballet during Armageddon. Perhaps we could make a stop in Minsk before heading back to Tallinn? Probably relieved by my lack of reportorial zeal, Andrus hastily nodded in agreement and proposed that we visit a former girlfriend of his who lived in a Soviet-era high-rise in west Moscow. We could have some tea and chat a bit and then continue our trek to Belarus.

One more tragedy was to await us as we made our way to Potapov's to thank him for his hospitality, collect our things, and say good-bye. Our car still stood unscathed in the courtyard, where, bizarrely, children were squealing and playing, as if life was absolutely normal and today was like any other day. We climbed the ill-shapen stairs to Potapov's floor, inhaling stale air that reeked of boiled cabbage, fried onions, and urine (whether animal or human I couldn't tell) and evading the water bugs and cockroaches on the walls. Funny, I thought, that I hadn't noticed the stench and the vermin before, but now, with thoughts of the apocalypse swirling in my besotted brain, my senses were sharpened and every flaw appeared magnified. Andrus unlocked the door and pushed it open. He called Potapov's name, but was met with silence.

"He's probably out," he said. "We'll have to write him a note. There's no time to wait. Is that okay?" The last sentence wasn't a question, so I grunted my assent and followed him into the living room.

There, sprawled out on the colorful peasant-style kilim, lay Potapov, his face blown away, his false teeth scattered and cracked, a gun lodged in what remained of his mouth still adorned, bizarrely, by bits of his mustache. Pinned to his chest was a note: *"Bolshe ne mogu. Moya strana umiraet."* "I cannot anymore. My country is dying." It took me several seconds to realize that he was dressed in his KGB uniform. The pants were neatly pressed, the jacket and shirt were free of any wrinkles or stains, and, most extraordinary, four rows of medals, all perfectly arrayed, were pinned to his chest. Obviously, Potapov had donned the outfit he wore only on exceptional days, laid down carefully, arranged the baubles that meant so much to him, pulled his head back, opened his mouth, and, placing his pistol-bearing hand diagonally across his chest, pulled the trigger.

I was transfixed by the ritualistic nature of the neatly dressed corpse's suicide and would have probably stayed there, staring, for a few more minutes, but the ever-practical Andrus pulled me into the room where we had slept—how he managed in light of my leaden feet and wooden bearing I do not know —and shut the door as quietly as possible. Remarkably, the scotch-induced wooziness that I had felt vanished and was replaced by an all-too-painful sobriety and fear.

"We must leave here immediately," Andrus ordered with a force that brooked no disagreement. "Take your things. I'll try to remove our fingerprints. Don't look so surprised, Steven. We are foreigners. His body may remain undiscovered for weeks.

The police may never regroup. But we are foreigners and Potapov was a former big fish with highly placed friends. We must be careful lest they begin looking for scapegoats and make us into foreign provocateurs." As he left the room with a washcloth, he added: "Everything is possible in this impossible country—especially as it is sliding into oblivion." I stood motionless for several minutes, uncertain of what to say and fearful of doing anything that could be construed as complicity in Potapov's death. The door creaked slightly as we exited, Andrus locked it, and, after we descended the stairs as noiselessly as we could, he threw the keys into a garbage container. "It's best that he remains undiscovered for several days," he explained. "By then, we'll be long gone and in safety."

The car didn't start immediately and, already sweating profusely, I responded with heart palpitations and clammy hands. Andrus instructed me to get out and push and, my shoes slipping and sliding along the greasy surface of the yard, I finally managed a shove and the engine—miraculously, so it seemed to me—ignited and I quickly jumped in, but not before knocking my forehead against the side mirror. We negotiated the narrow tunnel-like exit covered with obscene drawings of Pitun and racist graffiti and made a left and, after taking the streets with fewest pedestrians, we finally headed west for the high-rise with Andrus's ex-girlfriend.

I should have paid attention to the goings-on around me, but the pain in my head, the effects of an overabundance of alcohol, and the shock of seeing poor Potapov with his head blown off were too much for me. I shut my eyes and, while breathing deeply (Andrus asked whether I was okay and I nodded), I thought of our dead host. His world had collapsed twice—once in 1991, when the Soviet Union came to an end, and today, when Russia came to an end. His life's work had proven to be an illusion. Nothing was left of it. Others fled or pillaged. Potapov, being a man of genuine belief and commitment—I had wanted to say honor, but wasn't sure that his activities in the KGB had all been honorable—had no choice but to go down with the ship to which he had dedicated all his life.

I opened my eyes as the car slowed to a crawl. We were crossing a bridge on both sides of which scores of bound and blindfolded men were arrayed. Groups of boys armed with broom sticks and wrenches went down the rows and struck them on their heads, whereupon they either fell forward or were pushed into the river. "Probably Chechens," Andrus murmured. "Don't look, Steven! Just face forward and pretend that nothing unusual is going on. Here, have a cigarette. And, for heaven's sake, wipe that look of horror off your face! Do you want to join them?" It took some effort to do so, since each splash reminded me that Mother Russia's precious children had become savages.

CHAPTER TWO

Minsk and Tallinn

The area in which Natasha, Andrus's former paramour, lived consisted of monotonously arranged and even more monotonously constructed seven-story, raw brick buildings interspersed among what probably used to be green lawns and vibrant trees. The windows were adorned with variously-sized satellite dishes, the balconies were mostly enclosed and crammed with all manner of junk, and the entrances were framed by chipped concrete beams and featured heavy doors smeared with obscenities and anti-Pitun slogans. Here, even the outside reeked of cabbage, onions, and urine. How could, I thought, people live under conditions such as these? On the other hand, I had to admit that, in contrast to the central city, the housing complex exuded normality. Dowdy women in baggy coats and frayed kerchiefs sat on benches and gossiped, producing occasional yelps, cackles, and shrieks that mimicked laughter. Unshaven, red-faced men stood in clusters, smoking foul-smelling cigarettes. Indifferent to the protruding screws and decaying wood, blonde-haired children played on the rusty swings and creaking seesaws. The battlefields we had just witnessed could have been on a different planet.

Photographs of this quotidian ordinariness would be a nice counterpoint to the tragic thrust of my future stories, so I reached for my pocket and realized my camera was missing. I must have dropped it during the commotion on Red Square or, perhaps, while pushing the car. Normally, I would have cursed and kicked and screamed, but, feeling enervated by what we had just experienced, I only muttered a quiet damn and let the matter drop. Too bad, though, as I had taken some fabulous shots that would have saved me more than a thousand words of prose.

Natasha waved at us as from the second floor as we approached her building. Two flights of dirty and uneven stairs later, and we were welcomed by a diminutive and exceedingly busty woman with curly blond hair, a sizable mole on her right cheek, hastily applied red lipstick on her lips and teeth, and a fake-pearl necklace draped over an embroidered peasant shirt. She kissed Andrus three times and then embraced him until he turned beet red. A polite handshake with me followed, as Andrus told her exactly who I was and why we were here. She ushered us into the cramped living cum dining room (cum bedroom, I thought, as I espied the fold-out couch on one side of the table). The walls were draped with brightly colored Russian village kilims and genuinely old icons (which testified to some pull and lots of money) and the few remaining spaces were incongruously decorated with kitschy landscapes featuring thick globs of oil paint that mimicked leafy trees, the ripples on a lake, or the smoothness of stones. An old-fashioned, Stalin-era mahogany cabinet (that must have weighed a ton) full of dishes and knick-knacks stood in one corner. The floor was also covered with kilims. The overall effect was that of a prosperous peasant's abode on the eve of collectivization.

The table, unsurprisingly, was bedecked with food and drink, identical to that at Potapov's, but served with greater care and solicitude. We sat, we toasted, we drank, and then Andrus and Natasha reminisced, while I ate as much of the greasy fish and heavy bread as my abused innards could tolerate. By the time they had finished their nostalgic forays into what was surely an idealized and misremembered past, my head had ceased aching and my mind was clear—or clearer. The corpses and blood-spattered cobblestones seemed distant and I was in the mood for a decisive reassertion of my professional qualifications and some pointed questions.

"Madam," I opened with excessive formality in Russian

and saw from her smile that she was not displeased, "the center of Moscow resembles a battlefield, as I'm sure you know, while here everything seems to be perfectly normal. Are you not—"

"—afraid?" she interposed. "Of course, I am afraid. We all are. Don't let the banter and the smoking in the yards fool you. We are all aware of what is going on. Chaos—and it will get much worse before it gets better. We know that," she spoke with determination, not with uncertainty, "we Russians know that. We survived two wars, a revolution, we survived Stalin and Gorbachev and Yeltsin." She broke into a broad smile that revealed two gold teeth. "We will survive Pitun." And then, after brushing away several strands of hair: "And now, dear friends, eat."

It was Andrus's turn to eat and mine to speak, so I resumed my questions. "So, what, if I may ask, are your plans? How will you cope with the oncoming collapse of the polity, the economy, perhaps even the society? What if there is civil war? Or war? Right here in Moscow and not somewhere along the periphery?"

"You ask too many questions, *dorogoi* Styopa"—she had lapsed into the Russian diminutive, a good sign—"but, since you insist, here is my answer. We will survive just as we have always survived. By starving, by dying, by being humiliated, tortured, and robbed—and then, miraculously, by continuing to live. I see that my answer doesn't satisfy you, but that's because you, as an American, want details, technical details: what concrete steps will we take and so on, right? But the only concrete steps a Russian in Russia can take is to be Russian. And Russians, despite the hecatombs they have experienced—and imposed on others, I should add: do not worry, *dorogoi* Styopa, I am no chauvinist— always survive. And so will we." She stopped speaking briefly to survey my face. "And again, you are dissatisfied with my answer, but it is the only one I have."

She was right. I had hoped for details and she had given me a rousing campaign speech full of generalities. That said, she

was right. Russians, like their country, had an elephantine quality to them. They lumbered along, smashing and destroying
everything in their path, seemingly oblivious of what they were
doing, impervious to pain, impervious to wisdom, impervious
to knowledge, impervious to progress. One expected the beast
to drop dead and, no matter how often it fell to its knees and
seemed on the verge of extinction, it always managed to rise,
however awkwardly, however cumbersomely.

But this time, as Potapov sensed, things could be different. This time, the elephant might really be slaughtered. After
seeing what had transpired on Red Square, I was inclined to
trust Potapov's existential pessimism more than Natasha's cautious optimism. But I decided not to press the case. She believed what she believed and who was I to shake the belief that
sustained her in this time of troubles? Perhaps she was wrong,
perhaps her thinking was muddled, but I knew that belief gave
us great strength, which is exactly what she would need in the
weeks and months ahead, just as the sudden loss of belief, as Potapov's corpse attested, also led to an extraordinary weakness
that boded nothing but death.

The meal over, the reminiscences finished, further questions lacking, Andrus and I excused ourselves and—notwithstanding her formal protestations: she knew as well as we did
that it was high time for us to go—we repeated the ceremony
that accompanied our greeting and, after enquiring where we
might be able to get some gas, departed. Outside, in a kind of
déjà vu, she looked out the window and waved, while the knots
of men and women still occupied the same spaces and sat on the
same benches, gossiping and smoking and waiting calmly for
the end of the world.

*

The roads heading west were packed with cars, mostly foreign-
made sedans, but we were able to maintain a speed of about
thirty-to-forty miles per hour and reach the Belarusian border

just as the sun was rising behind our backs and casting long shadows onto the highway. I had slept, though fitfully and beset with disturbing dreams, for most of the time and had no idea how Andrus managed to stay on the road and get us to our destination. Perhaps the meeting with Natasha had awakened a plethora of pleasant (and unpleasant?) memories that fueled his wakefulness. Perhaps the full appreciation of the catastrophe that had befallen Estonia's immense neighbor, and the consequences that it might have for his country, had unsettled his nerves and provided the adrenalin he needed to stay awake. Whatever the case, we were almost out of immediate danger.

I rubbed my eyes and, espying the long line of vehicles stretched out before us, groaned, but, horn blaring, Andrus cursed Mother Russia with all the English-language expletives at his command, swiveled onto the grassy shoulder and, ignoring the waving fists and shouting that we were American diplomats, bypassed the queue and, beating all the odds, reached the border control point. The Belarusians had set up imposing coils of barbed wire on either side of the road and were carefully examining passports, letting some cars pass, while instructing most to turn back. The Russians, their faces red with anger and desperation, did so reluctantly, some arguing, some pleading, most ultimately accepting the inevitable in time-honored Russian style and bowing to their unhappy fate.

Fortunately, my U.S. passport and press card—my paper still carries some weight in most of the world—as well as the hundred-dollar bill I saw Andrus slip into the border guard's hand had the desired effect and, after thirty minutes of pointless waiting intended to show who was in charge, we were waved through. A stop for outrageously expensive gas—the Belarusians had obviously learned a thing or two about capitalism—and a bite to eat—I've always had a weak spot for Belarusian borscht—and a few hours later we registered in the Minsk Motel, a low-lying shabby Soviet-era construction located amid a forbidding forest some ten miles outside the city, where, despite the stained sheets, rusty water, brown soap, threadbare towels, and rollicking water bugs, we lay down on the uncomfortably soft mattresses and immediately fell asleep for a blissful three hours. I was up first and nudged Andrus. We quickly dressed, had a stale cheese sandwich and tea in the musty dining room attended by a bored waiter in a stained maroon vest, and set out for the Belarusian capital. One hour later, we were in downtown Minsk, having driven past the statue of Lenin and parked in one of the side streets in the bit of the city that hadn't been destroyed in the war.

I had been in Minsk once before, many years ago, but Andrus visited it often, apparently having some shady business dealings, about which he preferred to be silent, with nameless individuals who traded Russian gas—which, I thought, probably accounted for the Rolex he liked to sport on the streets of Tallinn (but not now: now he wore a cheap Chinese watch that probably cost three dollars). We took the main street, a broad thoroughfare that cut the city in two and was lined with Stalin-era wedding cake buildings similar to those in Kyiv, Moscow, and the former East Berlin. In stark contrast to Moscow's harried inhabitants, the Belarusians seemed to be in no particular hurry; nor did their faces evince any exceptional stress.

"It seems to be business as usual," I said to Andrus, who, seeing the look of disappointment on my face, shook his head and said that the Belarusians had learned to live with crisis—they had, he noted, lost a third of their population during the war—by maintaining straight faces that betrayed as little emotion as possible.

"Don't be fooled," he cautioned, "they haven't forgotten the mass marches that almost brought down Lukashenka and they know exactly what is happening in Russia." A pause and then, almost as an afterthought: "They are terrified of what it portends for them."

"Russian refugees?"

"Yes," he answered, "but Pitun's end could also spell the end of Belarus's own dictator and that, in turn, could mean a power struggle, civil conflict, and, heaven help them, chaos."

"I thought they wanted to get rid of him."

"Of course, they do. It's all a question of how. No one here wants a civil war." My thoughts turned to the devastation on Red Square and I nodded.

After a few seconds of awkward silence, Andrus turned to me and confided: "I have some, er, friends in the energy sector. They have level heads and are always exceedingly well informed about—er, about everything." He removed his cell phone and pressed a speed dial button. "Let's see if Zianon Bykau is available. He speaks good English and is a Belarusian nationalist. I think you'll like him." A few rings later, a deep voice answered the phone and, after a brief exchange of pleasantries, Andrus agreed to a meeting with the Belarusian. "Let's go," Andrus ordered. "Bykau is expecting us immediately." The man was probably a gangster, I thought, but, as a source, his credentials were sure to be impeccable.

*

Bykau occupied a corner table in a high-end restaurant outfitted with intimate red-satin booths, mirrors galore, and an army of large-leafed plants whose reflections appeared to recede into infinity. I was expecting someone of Andrus's general appearance, but Bykau was tall and lanky and had a full head of slightly graying blond hair, a clean-shaven pale face, a thin nose, and deep-set crystalline blue eyes. In a word, he was handsome and, fully aware of his good looks, exuded confidence and authority, perhaps even charisma. His grip was powerful and he pumped my hand longer than necessary in a transparent attempt to establish his primacy. He would, I saw, be an interesting interlocutor, especially as his English was, like Andrus's, almost free of any accent. That could bespeak a facility for languages, success at business, or, less cheerfully, a KGB past.

"Would you like something to eat?" He looked up inquisitively from his plate. "The steak is excellent. They can even prepare it medium rare and seared Pittsburgh style. My personal favorite; reminds me of the States." I was surprised by his knowledge of such culinary technicalities and noticed that he had just begun eating a huge Porterhouse. Andrus and I exchanged glances and nodded, whereupon Bykau motioned to a waitress and ordered two more of the same.

"You won't regret it," he added. "Beer? Wine? Vodka?"

"We'll have whatever you're having," I suggested.

"*Devushka!*" he shouted, "*eshche vodochki dlya moikh druzey.*" No more than thirty seconds later, the girl brought the diminutive vodka he had ordered for his friends. Bykau, I saw, had pull and he obviously enjoyed displaying it, just as he enjoyed flashing the gold rings on four of his fingers.

"And now, my friends—you don't mind if I continue eating? This piece of excellent meat will otherwise get cold—and that would be a crying shame. So, what can I do for you?"

I let Andrus respond with a brief, though accurate, account of what we had seen in Moscow. He concluded with a glance in my direction, almost as if he were asking for my permission, and the statement that "the Russians appear to think —"

"Not appear," I corrected him.

"Yes," he glided over my interruption, "the Russians think that it is the end."

"The end of what?" Bykau, who had been eating all this time, looked up from his plate.

"Of Russia," I said. "Of Russia the state, of Russia the country, of Russia the embodiment of Pitun."

"They are right," he said nonchalantly, almost as if he were commenting on manifestly beautiful weather. "My colleagues and I—my good friend Andrus has told you what business we are in, yes?—have been expecting something like this for years." He stopped chewing and quietly placed fork and knife on the plate. "It's very simple, at least from a businessman's point of view. You cannot spend more than you make, not in the long run. If you do, you go belly up, yes? The Russians have been spending and expanding far more than their decrepit economy could sustain. It was only a matter of time before the house of cards built by Comrade Pitun came tumbling down. Like Jack and Jill, yes?" He reengaged his steak and watched delightedly as ours arrived. "Dig in!" he encouraged us unnecessarily.

"Very well," I said, "it is the end. But the country won't just disappear. Neither will the people. What happens next?"

"More of the same," he answered drily, almost as if he were bored by the obviousness of it all. "More war, more civil war, more killings, more assassinations, more bombings—until at some point the chaos will bring forth another tsar who will impose a semblance of order on the country. But," he sniffed, "that could take decades and, until it happens, I would not invest in that unhappy country. But I would divest myself A-sap of all my holdings there." That last suggestion was obviously directed at Andrus.

"The refugees—and there could be millions—will come to Belarus. What then?"

"That, my friends, is why God created barbed wire, yes? You saw our border, yes? Were the Russians streaming in like a flood? No, because our wise and eternal leader—God bless him and his devotion to hockey—ordered that we keep that fraternal nation out." He looked mischievously at Andrus. "I bet they'll go to Estonia. And Latvia. You are members of the great European Union and must, alas, abide by—what do they call them?—ah, yes, European values. You must be humane and take in political and religious refugees. We barbarians of the last dictatorship in Europe need not be so charitable." His eyes were gleaming, almost twinkling, as he added with unvarnished irony: "Sometimes, it is good to be a brute, yes?"

"And, in the meantime, what happens to Russian energy exports? And to energy traders like yourself?"

He eyed me suspiciously. "I see that our friend Andrus has been doing his job conscientiously and has briefed you, but"—he turned to Andrus—"not, I trust, bored you with too many technical details." Andrus shook his head vigorously as Bykau finished the sentence. "That, my friends, will not change. Russia may be in freefall, but the oligarchs with fancy apartments in London and New York will not permit the spigots to shut. The gas and oil will continue to flow, the pipelines will continue to be guarded against terrorism—but by private militias, warlords in the pay of our dear oligarchs—and honest businessmen like me"—he purposely snorted as he spoke these words—"will continue to profit. Oh, and yes, Germany and all the other kind, sweet, dear European defenders of human rights will continue to heat their homes with energy from a totalitarian land. You see, my friends, it is a win-win-win all around! We brutes get money—filthy lucre is how you call it, yes?—and the righteous Europeans get heat. A perfect match! One made in heaven."

"Or hell," I opined.

Bykau replied with a prolonged loud laugh. "Or hell, he says! Or hell! You know, Andrusha, I really like this guy. Or hell!" A sudden cough put a temporary end to his exclamations, but, after imbibing an entire glass of water, he resumed with his outsized display of enthusiasm for my two-word sentence. "You know, Mister Steven, you are no doubt wondering what is so funny about what you just said. Very little, actually, but you will permit me this outbreak of gallows humor. Hell, Mister Steven"—he was tapping the table with his fork—"hell, Mister Steven, is not just Russia today. It is every day here and there and everywhere."

The tapping stopped. "You know, Mister Steven, I am a nationalist—I use that word purposefully: after all, it is far too easy to be a weak-kneed patriot who claims to love his country. But I, Mister Steven, I love this nation. I love my people and I love Belarus. Not just any country, but *this* country, this *Belarusian* country. You may not believe me, Mister Steven, but I will do everything I need to do to defend my motherland—and if that means keeping fraternal Russians out, despite their excessive love for this land and its miserable inhabitants, then so be it. If that means shooting at them, because of their excessive love for us, then so be it. If that means profiting from their avarice, which, as you no doubt know, is as deep as the taiga is wide, then so be it." He pushed the plate away and drank a glassful of vodka. "Their death is our life. It is that simple."

"Hear, hear," Andrus proclaimed almost inaudibly, though conclusively. Our steaks had been devoured, the conversation was at any obvious end, so Bykau paid the check—"You are my guests. Please hide your wallets or I shall be deeply insulted"—and, after whispering something in Andrus's ear and pumping my hand, he did an about-face and left us standing near the table, somewhat bewildered by his impetuous behavior.

"Is he angry at you?" I asked hesitantly, recalling the scowl Bykau had directed at him.

"The whispering? Oh, no, not at all. We are old friends who are also indispensable business partners. Zianon knows I would never betray him and I know he would never betray me. Partly because we trust each other and mostly because we could destroy each other's careers. As to the whisper, he said we should leave the city as soon as possible. There are, he said, reliable rumors that the president will declare a state of emergency and close the borders. Don't look so alarmed, Steven. Belarus is quite a pleasant place and its trains always run on time, but, I agree, we would be well advised to skedaddle." I couldn't resist a smile at his use of so silly a word, though I suspect he believed it was a smile of relief.

Tallinn was in an uproar. The armed forces had been mobilized, volunteer units had sprung up throughout the country and were marching in the streets, singing the national anthem and waving flags, women organized emergency medical services, and school children were dismissed from class along with instructions that they should take refuge in basements if aerial bombardments took place. Blue, black, and white flags hung from most windowsills. The country was ready for an invasion —though whether it would be led by soldiers or refugees wasn't clear. The change in mood was strikingly inappropriate, almost comically so. When I had first arrived here, the invasion had actually taken place, but Tallinn was peaceful. Now that the Russians were in full retreat, Tallinn was readying itself for an invasion.

Riina, Andrus's slim, Nordic-looking wife, greeted us with tears in her reddened eyes and, after embracing Andrus, scolded him for not calling as often as he had promised. He countered with the ring he had purloined in the GUM and, squealing with delight after asking whether it was real gold, she forgave him his inconsiderate behavior and pressed him into a chair. I asked if I could recluse myself in some corner of the apartment—I had to write my stories—and left them to their intimacies and whisperings. Having experienced so much in so short a time, I was bursting with energy and banged out three, to my mind excellent, stories in a few hours. The words flowed, as they sometimes do, and, upon rereading the texts, I found that I had very few corrections to make. They were ready to go. I sent the files to my editor and sat back in my chair.

Now what? Should I stay here? Or should I go—and, if so, where? To New York? What would I see here that I hadn't already seen? Well, frankly, a lot. Who knew how chaos would unfold? It was quite possible that the next few days or weeks could witness some utterly different developments—and it behooved me as a journalist to be on the spot. On the other hand, I had already filed three stories (or was it four?). For the time being, my work was done. Moreover, I was emotionally and physically drained by the bloodshed and mayhem, but also by the ceaseless running about. I had, I calculated, gotten an absurdly small number of hours of sleep while imbibing more than my share of hard liquor. Why not take a rest and see how things unfolded? Returning to New York made no sense, but someplace in Europe —someplace I could relax a bit and cleanse my mind of the horrific images that beset it—just might.

The Riviera, which I knew well and loved, was the obvious choice. It was beautiful. The food was excellent. I could swim a bit and the peripatetic Russians there could keep me abreast of goings-on in their homeland, should I feel the need to consort with them. I hadn't been in Nice in a while. I'd go there for a few days and, if I needed to cut my vacation short, I could easily hop a plane and be back in Tallinn or Moscow or anywhere in the former Soviet Union in a few hours. That settled it. I would go to Nice. But not immediately, of course. A few days in Tallinn, a city that I had always found to be quite appealing and full of amenities, would serve as a nice transition to the Mediterranean charms of the south of France.

My Estonian hosts were still chatting in the kitchen, so, after informing Andrus of my plans (he approved), I decided to visit a watering hole near the city hall that was favored by foreign journalists. I certainly wasn't the only one of my breed in town and it could be useful, as well as pleasant, to meet some familiar faces and exchange some war stories. I ambled along the cobblestone streets and, a few blocks later, I stumbled upon the mayoralty. I first tried the street to its right, but found nothing. I had better luck in the curved alley to its left. I didn't recognize the place, but knew I had found it when a German correspondent, Hans von something-or-other, stumbled out of a doorway completely blotto and almost knocked me over.

The dark interior hid the faces, but some voices shouted "Steverino!" and, after my eyes adjusted, I recognized several boisterous colleagues in a booth and waved hello to them. They called on me to join them, but, with their sobriety being alarmingly low, I decided against it, at least until I could approximate their blood-alcohol levels, and went to the bar and ordered a gin and tonic. Upon hearing my voice, the bony brunette with the oversized mouth and aquiline nose to my left turned toward me and, speaking in husky undertones, said, "Greetings, stranger, long time no see. Welcome to the end of the world." It was, of all people, Pippa Tumblethwaite, a British correspondent for one of their major London papers and an old friend with whom, despite our frequent meetings and incessant flirtations—due, in all likelihood, to her sultry voice and languid eyes, both of which conveyed an almost irresistibly seductive charm—I had never shared, or wanted to share, a bed. It was strictly business for the preposterously named Pippa, but, more important, it was also strictly business for me.

We exchanged our impressions of Russia. She had just come in from St. Petersburg and was as shocked by the chaos enveloping the city as I had been with respect to Moscow. The Hermitage had been bombed and destroyed. Even the Winter Palace had been reduced to a pile of ashes, presumably by Chechens with an anti-Bolshevik streak. The population had taken to pillaging; official buildings were set on fire, by Russians no less, and all semblance of order had disappeared—as had the local authorities, presumably to Helsinki by means of their private boats. She was, she announced, *completely* fatigued. Her stay, like mine, had been short, but the sight of a collapsing civilization had exhausted her. I said I felt the same way and intended to leave for a short vacation to Nice. Her eyebrows, which usually hovered motionlessly above her impressive proboscis and luxuriant mouth, shot up and she asked if she might join me.

"Separate rooms, of course, ducky," she added unnecessarily, "as well as separate checks." Why not? I thought. She was amusing and wouldn't be a burden. Indeed, I'd probably see very little of her and it would be nice to share breakfast or an evening drink.

"Sure," I replied and told her what flight I'd be taking. "There were many unoccupied seats, so you shouldn't have any problems." We shook hands and closed the deal. I said good-bye, sauntered over to the besotted colleagues in the booth, told them a joke, slapped a few backs, and then made for home.

My head was clear, so I drank a beer in Andrus's kitchen and, tip-toing past the sleeping couple (they were sprawled on the sofa, both snoring), retired to my room, which is to say, their bedroom. The thought of Pippa accompanying me to Nice gave me no rest. It had seemed like a good enough idea a few hours ago, but now I wondered. She could be as insistent and humorless as she could be easy-going and funny. Would we get along? Wouldn't we quarrel about some insignificant detail over which neither of us, being pig-headed as well as highly paid journalists, was willing to budge, as we usually did?

And then there was always the danger, hanging above us like the sword of Damocles, of a romantic entanglement. There is, I well knew from bitter experience, little worse, little more complicated, and little more resembling a Gordian Knot— apologies for the mixed metaphors, but that's my classical edu-cation speaking—than a relationship with a journalist. We were demanding, hurried, irascible, impatient, competitive, egotis-tical, crude, rude, and perpetually besotted. Such assignations always ended and they always ended in embarrassing blow-ups in public places that required the utmost self-control lest the manager be impelled to throw one out. I felt no particular attraction to Pippa—her surname was such an absurd tongue-twister that I could never have countenanced a relationship with her—but accidents did happen. Little Cupid could send one of his arrows in my direction and I could, fully unaware of the projectile's velocity, step into its path. On the other hand, wasn't I overdramatizing things? Three days in Nice were hardly enough time to take a dip in the sea and take a stroll along the shore. And it would surely be insufficient time for more than a few quarrels to be had. Yes, I decided, all would be well—why shouldn't it?—and, after some desultory tossing and turning, I finally fell asleep.

*

I awoke to the mellifluous voice of a television broadcaster. My hosts were fully dressed and sitting at the table, eating breakfast, sipping coffee, and watching Estonian news. A third cup and plate awaited me, so I joined them and, after seeing tanks roll across the screen, asked Andrus what was going on. The Ukrainians, he announced, had broken through the Russian lines in the Donbas and were now moving their mechanized units toward the Kuban, a grain-rich territory that had historically been inhabited by Ukrainian speakers. The Russian army had fallen back chaotically and the road to Stavropol, the Kuban's main city, was open. Analysts expected Ukrainian forces to occupy the city in no more than a day or two.

Meanwhile, in the Far East, Chinese tanks had attacked Russian positions along the Ussuri River, the site of fierce clashes between Soviet and Chinese forces in 1969. They were, so the Chinese, reclaiming their long-lost historical territories. The Chinese migrants living in that part of the Russian Federation—there appeared to be hundreds of thousands, possibly millions, who had gone there for jobs—had proven to be a reliable fifth column, having strung up local Russian officials from street lamps and encouraged the Russian population to pack their bags and head westward.

A cascade of declarations of independence was also taking place. Sakha-Yakutia, Tatarstan, Bashkortostan, Chechnya, Ingushetia all issued solemn statements that proclaimed their complete and total separation from the Russian Federation and their longed-for return to the community of free nations. China, America, and the United Kingdom extended official recognition to them and said they'd be setting up embassies and sending ambassadors as soon as conditions permitted. The United Nations General Assembly issued a ringing declaration in their support.

"Potapov was right," Andrus said in between bites of a sugary pastry. "Though I still can't comprehend that it's all falling apart in a few days." He shook his head solemnly. "And to think that most *experts*"—he spoke the word with unconcealed disdain—"believed Pitun's rule would be eternal…"

"We always make that mistake," I said. "We project what is into the future, because that's easier to imagine than its negation. Same thing happened with the Soviet Union. Remember? Everyone was in shock."

"We weren't," he countered, "not the Estonians. But who listens to a Lilliputian people with a long memory?" He switched channels to the BBC. Several experts, nicely balanced for sex, age, and skin color, were debating what happened to Pitun. Why did he jump ship so quickly? Where was he? Would he mount a counterattack? The general opinion was that he was finished and was probably in hiding someplace in Europe or North America. "The man stole at least seventy-five billion dollars," a British academic claimed. "He'll be where his assets and money are." London? New York? Palm Beach? The Cayman Islands? Paris? Cyprus? They went down the list of possible havens for Russia's formerly extraordinary great Leader (his megalomaniacal designation, not mine) and couldn't agree on any one place as being the obvious choice for a man of supposedly simple tastes, deep pockets, and no moral qualms.

Should he be hunted down by Interpol and tried in The Hague? The moderator asked. The unanimous answer was *yes*, but the experts also said they expected no such thing to happen. Pitun had hobnobbed for decades with the high and mighty of the whole world. Everyone—every celebrity, every statesman and -woman, every politician, every general—had shaken his hand, laughed at his jokes, praised his rule, lauded his wisdom, and ignored his crimes. In a word, they had all morally collaborated with him and were very unlikely to cry for the blood of a man who could embarrass them or, quite possibly, even have them arrested. Either way, their careers would be over. "That being the case," a female journalist from South Africa added, "hands will be wrung, tears will be shed, declarations will be issued, but every effort will be made to keep Pitun safely out of the public eye and hidden beneath the rug."

"European values will triumph once again," Riina said with all-too-obvious sarcasm, a cigarette dangling provocatively, Camus-like, from between her lips.

"They always do," Andrus replied matter-of-factly, "especially when they clash with self-interest."

"And they *always* clash with self-interest."

The astringent bitterness with which they spoke outdid even the awful taste of the unpotable coffee. A change of mood was desirable, lest my hosts began engaging in the kind of despairing criticism and self-criticism for which Estonians, like all the Nordic peoples forced to spend so much of the year in total darkness, were famous, so I asked what, if any, our plans for today were.

"There is a Russian refugee camp someplace between Tartu and Lake Peipus," Andrus replied, his eyes having regained their usual luster. "Would you like to visit it? We could be there in two hours, maybe less." He looked apologetic and at a momentary loss for words. "I'm sorry, Steven, had I known about the camp, we could have visited it on the way from Minsk. It would've meant a very slight detour."

"No problem," I assured him. "Besides, I don't pay you to know everything, just—"

"—almost everything." He laughed, shaking his head in overstated incredulity. "You Americans..."

*

We found the camp easily: ten rows of about twenty capacious tents in a placid meadow. The lake shimmered in the distance. A simple chain-link fence bordered the tents on three sides, more to create an impression of order than to keep anyone in or out. Several obviously bored soldiers were posted at the entrance, near which stood a makeshift cottage that housed the officials in one room and served as a field hospital in another. My press pass worked its magic and, after Andrus exchanged a few words in Estonian with an officer, we made our way into the settlement. Most of the Russians were outside, the women in their groups, the men in theirs, the children playing. I was immediately struck by their faces. Gone were the worried frowns, the looks of horror, the animal fear. These people knew they were in safety and looked unperturbed, almost self-assured.

We approached one group of men, excused and introduced ourselves, and, before lighting up, offered them cigarettes. They were all friends, workers in the same factory, and hailed from Pskov, which lay just beyond the border. Do you know it? One of them asked. I shook my head. A beautiful city, he intoned mournfully, an old Russian city—one of the oldest. Another chimed in proudly: we're older than Moscow and Peter. And we have our own Kremlin and many churches. It's a great city, a third one added and then his voice trailed off.

"So, why did you leave? Why not stay and weather this crisis?"

The eldest of the lot, gray-haired and with a wrinkled face that resembled worn-out corduroy, inhaled deeply, lifted his face to the heavens, as if he were expecting a divine intervention, and beat his chest with both fists—not Tarzan-style, but as a seeming act of contrition. "When the German fascists came, we fought. When Napoleon came, we also fought. But when the Mongols attacked in the thirteenth century, when they destroyed every living thing in their path, we ran." He screwed up his eyes as the smoke rose from the cigarette lodged securely between his leathery lips. "Have you seen who is attacking us now?" He didn't wait for me to answer. "The Mongols, the slant-eyes, the Asian barbarians. They are like locusts," he nodded sadly, "they are like damned locusts."

"But what of your brothers, the Ukrainians and the Belarusians?" I interjected. "They have also turned against you."

My anodyne statement of what I took to be an obvious fact provoked a stormy response. "Propaganda and lies," he roared, "*filthy* propaganda and *dirty* lies. I do not believe it." The others nodded in assent. "We are three branches of one people and they love us as much as we love them." The last statement obviously brooked no dissent, so, with Andrus gently tugging on my sleeve, I nodded solemnly and wished them all the best.

"A close call, Steven. You must learn to restrain your journalistic impulses sometimes. That man was ready to devour you."

Andrus was right, so I smiled weakly and decided to change the subject. "What's next for these folks? Will Estonia take them?"

"*Take them?*" he asked incredulously. "Don't be absurd, my friend. Like all good Europeans who are committed to European values, we will do everything possible to make their stay in Estonia safe and comfortable and then we will do everything possible to ship them to the country that embodies those very same values—fraternal Germany. It is a big, rich country and they have room."

"And if the Germans refuse?"

"They won't. They're too German to do that. But," and now his eyes were visibly twinkling, "if by some miracle they do, we will attest to the folkish German origins of all our dear Russians and insist that Germany repatriate its countrymen and women." We had reached the gate and waved good-bye to the officers and soldiers. "If appealing to their humanity doesn't work, we will appeal to their nationalism. That always works."

We stopped in Tartu for a late lunch. Andrus proposed a little Ukrainian restaurant near the university; its food was hearty and, since the place was favored by an impoverished student clientele, its prices were cheap. "Taras" (I wasn't sure whether it was named after Gogol's Cossack hero, Bulba, or after Ukraine's national poet, Shevchenko) was more of a cafeteria than a bona fide restaurant, but the aromas were welcoming and the tables, which came with Coke bottles containing a little blue-and-yellow Ukrainian flag alongside an Estonian one, were almost all occupied. Both of us ordered borscht and potato dumplings with sour cream, melted butter, and fried onions. We ate in silence, in sharp contrast to the other customers, who were clinking their vodka glasses and singing what I took to be Ukrainian patriotic songs. Or are they yours? I asked Andrus. No, he said, they're Ukrainian.

The festive atmosphere was presumably due to the Ukrainian army's rapid advances in southern Russia. After decades of being one-upped and humiliated by Russia, Ukrainians were finally having their revenge and obviously enjoying it. I could well imagine that there was dancing and singing in the streets of Kyiv, which, despite resolutely speaking Russian, hated the Russians—a paradox that I could never quite fathom. And if the Ukrainians were celebrating Russia's end, I could just imagine how many champagne bottles were being uncorked all around the former Soviet Union.

It was payback time for all the non-Russians the Kremlin had, arguably since the fifteenth century, dominated, exploited, murdered, and exterminated. Payback time also meant bloodletting, but I doubted that Russia's exploited and downtrodden non-Russian peoples had excessive qualms about shedding the blood of their colonizers. Frantz Fanon's classic tract, *The Wretched of the Earth*, came to mind. His terrifying argument, that the native could only regain his humanity by exercising violence against the colonizer, had always struck me as morally muddled and politically self-defeating (even if psychologically liberating), especially as the toad-like denizen of Parisian cafés, Jean-Paul Sartre, heartily endorsed and enthusiastically promoted it over coffee and croissants, but I had no doubt of its appeal, and not just to Africans and Asians.

Andrus brought me back to reality with a slight nudge. "Look, they're doing a Crimean Tatar dance." Three slim, svelte girls with inky eyes and braided black hair were moving languorously in the center of the café, their hands flowing like gulls through the air, their fingers snapping, their feet shuffling soundlessly. The performance lasted several minutes and then two students with brush-like mustaches and shaven heads with long locks of hair—"They're Ukrainians," Andrus pointed out, "made out as Cossacks"—sprang from their seats and began doing a vigorous *hopak*, squatting, kicking up their legs, and punctuating their energetic movements with shouts of "Hey."

"They're celebrating." Andrus's comment was redundant. "All of us are."

"You really hate the Russians, don't you?"

He smiled weakly, almost as if he were forcing himself to do so. "No, not quite, although I would never say we love them. They're perfectly fine people and we know that. It's"— he seemed to be searching for the right word—"it's something else." He fell silent for a few seconds and then resumed. "When they're with us—Estonians, Ukrainians, Crimean Tatars, Chechens, whoever—when they're with us, they are boors, violent, insulting, aggressive boors. But, to be honest, Steven, I can accept that. What drives me and so many of us crazy is when the Russians try to be nice. Then they are insufferably condescending, as if they were our big brothers—you know, that's how they used to refer to themselves—bringing culture to the benighted masses.

"Can you believe that, Steven? *They* are bringing culture to *us*! If one knows anything about our history and theirs—and you do, of course—one sees just how absurd such a claim is. And yet, the ignorant, arrogant Russians cannot imagine themselves as not being in the center of the universe. So, am I happy that Russia is dying? I am delighted. And I fearful for the future? Yes, because, while it's true that we will all be able to breathe more easily now, it is also true that the wily Russian bear is exceedingly hard to kill. And I fear that bear. We all do." He took a deep breath. "But, in the meantime, there is cause to celebrate." At that, Andrus leaped from the table and joined a group of students doing a dance in which they placed their arms on one another's shoulders and, their feet moving rapidly forwards and backwards, went in a circle with shouts of "Hey" punctuating the rhythmic beat of their shoes.

As the festivities acquired an increasingly feverish momentum, I retreated into my cogitations. There was, I supposed, no liberation without bloodshed. The American colonists had gladly spilled British blood and were happy to spill their own. It was only a matter of how much bloodshed and whose. But those were reservations that were easy to have from outside, where one could split differences and count the number of angels on a moral pinhead. Once you were inside, once you faced do-or-die situations, these moral reservations and ethical niceties must seem scholastic at best and harmful at worst. The Chechens started the ball rolling with their bombings. One by one, the other nations joined them and, now that Russia was visibly on its last legs, even the reluctant, skittish nations were taking up real or verbal arms and joining the fight. Russia was licked. It could fight back against the hard-core nationalists willing to sacrifice their lives for the cause, but it couldn't defeat entire nations. The three Crimean Tatar girls and the two Ukrainians were proof of that. They would not stop dancing anymore. So much was clear even to a complete outsider like me.

When we arrived in Tallinn, Riina greeted us with news of four claimants to power in Russia. One of Pitun's less odious sidekicks had declared that he was acting as interim president.

He claimed to be in control of the Kremlin and to have the support of the security service, the FSB. Fat chance, I thought. A stocky bemedaled general someplace in the Urals claimed he had control of nuclear weapons and would—God and the people willing—use them to drive back the non-Russian hordes and reestablish a great and glorious Russia. That seemed far more likely. An oppositionist who had just been released from a Moscow prison claimed to be the voice of the people. Yeah, right. Finally, a government-in-exile consisting of three aging Russian ex-dissidents boarded a plane in London and disembarked in St. Petersburg, bringing good tidings of an imminent democratic Russia that would find its place in the European home. I had to laugh at their overblown ambitions.

It was, I thought, 1917-1921 again. Up to now, Russia had experienced non-Russian terrorism and war along with its own homegrown chaos. Now, it would descend into civil war. The four contenders—and there were going to be many more in the months ahead—would fight one another to the finish. Millions would die and the destruction initiated by the Chechens and others would be consummated by the Russians. All four aspirants sounded like tin pots to me. The only one who was a genuine source of concern was the general. If he truly had nuclear weapons and if he truly was mad enough to use them, then a world war involving a score of Russia's neighbors was no longer out of the question—not to mention the millions who might be incinerated in the blasts. It was probably bluster, but at a time like this one could never be quite sure. Perhaps I should stay here, after all? Wasn't that my duty as a journalist? Maybe yes, maybe no. Either way, I knew I needed a break from the end of the world and, notwithstanding my pangs of conscience, would leave as planned and, if necessary, come back refreshed and strengthened. Besides, if 1917-1921 were a guide to Russia's future, the turmoil would last several years and there would be ample time to write the definitive story of Russia's collapse.

*

Pippa was already waiting at the airport when I arrived. Dressed in tight jeans and a smart lime-green leather jacket, she greeted me with a wan smile and stuffed a paperback—it looked like a cheap airport detective mystery—into her pocket. Like good journalists, both of us had small carry-on suitcases and shoulder bags for our computers and we passed quickly through security and, without much ado, boarded a plane for Frankfurt, where we would catch a connecting flight to Nice. Some five hours later, the machine circled above the glistening Mediterranean and landed with a few bumps. The weather was perfect, of course, and, as we stepped outside the terminal and felt the warm air envelop us, I knew that I had done the right thing in coming here. We took a cab to the hotel, a modest three-star establishment on the Boulevard Victor Hugo, registered, and went to our rooms.

The two flights had been uneventful, though not uninteresting. I had never spent any time with Pippa outside a bar or press conference, so the experience of sitting next to a preposterously named Englishwoman in a tranquil setting was novel. Since she consumed several drinks during the first leg of our journey, Pippa probably felt as jittery as I was. I broke the ice by asking her about her surname. She produced an embarrassed smirk and proceeded to state that it was an exceedingly old family with some very indirect connections to some offshoot of the royal line. A great-grandfather or great-great-grandfather had been a baronet, "a rather fetching fellow judging from his portrait," but he loved to gamble and carouse with loose women and spent his fortune and died in some cheap hotel in Ostend, where his creditors couldn't get at him. Since then, the family had been resolutely middle class, with shopkeepers, merchants, and a scholar or two as the norm. "Margaret Thatcher would have fancied us and our values. We were the backbone of England, ducky."

There was one pitch-black sheep in the family, an uncle who had joined the Communist Party and served as a factory agitator. Pippa got along with him famously, not because of his politics, for which she had little understanding, but because he annoyed the rest of the family. Upon entering Cambridge—because of its legacy of harboring Reds and fellow travelers—she developed into a veritable firebrand opposed to everything that good taste deemed good, but, after a few desultory affairs, one with a married professor of classics, she got tired of opposing everything and decided to seek a profession that would enable her to retain her curiosity about the world and continue in her favored role as an outsider.

"What else could I do other than become a correspondent?" There were some ups, there were some downs—"you know them as well as I do"—and "here I am." She concluded with a broad smile and instantly swallowed the rest of her drink. "How about you, ducky? What's your story?"

"Haven't any," I said. "Mayflower, Connecticut WASP, sailboat, country clubs, penny loafers, lime-green Polo shirts, private school, Yale, majored in classics—"

"You read Greek and Latin?"

"I can even recite the first hundred lines of the *Aeneid*: '*Arma virumque cano*—'"

"Lovely, splendid, bravo—enough," she shook her head vigorously. "But for heaven's sake, *why?*"

"And you should hear me do Homer." I was determined to assert my irrelevance, at least for a few more seconds, and go down swinging.

"Yes, but why, Steven, *why?*"

"Both mother and father were classicists—she did Greece, he did Rome—so I followed in their footsteps."

"They encouraged you?"

"Actually, no. It, well, just seemed like the logical thing to do." Slightly embarrassed by my admission, I added, "So much for logic."

"Siblings?"

"None. Anyway, after I did my Master's, it was either the family business, the CIA"—I watched her eyebrows rise—"or writing, which I did fairly well—perhaps as a result of years of deciphering obscure texts. Come to think of it, it was the only thing I did fairly well. My great American novel failed, however —I couldn't find an agent or a publisher—so I went for Plan B. I had some connections, made a few phone calls, and presto, like you, here I am."

"Boring," she yawned. "At least I had a Red relative."

"Yeah, but my relatives worked in the OSS and helped found the CIA. Your uncle failed—hah! My uncles saved the free world." Would she get the irony? I could see from her giggle that she did.

"Is Russia your beat now?"

"More like the former Soviet Union and Eastern Europe and any other place they want to send me. As you know, we used to have correspondents in all the major capitals. Now, it's me and a few others. We live in the States and they send us wherever there's a story. Cheaper than living abroad."

"Journalism is not what it used to be," she observed sadly.

"Yeah, now they actually expect us to put in a nine-to-five day!"

We continued our banter for the duration of both flights. The vacation, I concluded, would not be a disaster. We actually managed to get along, at least when we weren't being journalists. Nice might even prove to be restful.

Just before we landed, she looked at me pensively and wondered what I was thinking about. I lied and said it was about what we had just seen in Russia.

CHAPTER THREE

Nice

As we met in the lobby, I said, "Today is Sunday," with the amazement of someone who had stumbled on buried treasure. "How can it possibly be Sunday? Where did the rest of the week go?" Time had become meaningless these last few days and I had lost my usually fastidious ability to navigate and utilize every minute of the week.

"Forgot, ducky? An early onslaught of dementia?" she quipped. "I have just the cure, love. We're going to Saint Nicholas Russian Orthodox Church. It's a few blocks away and we should just make it for the end of the service. Now, now, Steven, don't look so disappointed. You could use a bit of God. Besides, there's a tolerable little seafood bistro on the promenade where we can have a decent lunch afterward."

I made a gloomy face. "It's just that I was hoping not to meet any Russians for a while, and certainly not before a nice meal. I need a break from them." She nodded sympathetically, but didn't budge. "Still, Nice has always crawled with them, so we may as well go into the belly of the beast." I mirrored her forced smile. "And it could be interesting, I suppose. Wasn't it built by one of the tsars?"

Nodding, Pippa pushed me gently out the door and, while I was momentarily distracted by the swaying palm leaves, bright blue sky, and glistening asphalt, continued with what she probably hoped was infectious enthusiasm. "Russian émigrés are a fascinating lot, you know. They'd infested much of Western Europe—and especially its sunny climes—since the eighteenth century. Always scheming, always plotting—I'll take you to Alexander Herzen's grave later on: you *do* know who he is?—and always living cheerless lives which were pale shadows of what they once had and hoped to restore. Very moving, you know, but in a pathetic kind of way." She gave me a poke in the ribs. "Like you. We go left."

The crowds were just spilling out of the magnificent onion-domed structure—I couldn't help but think of St. Basil's Cathedral, lying prostrate in Red Square—when we stepped into the square. Some of the church-goers, presumably local inhabitants, were well-dressed; most looked shabby, as if they had just arrived after three days in a stuffy second-class Russian train compartment. The sour smell of unwashed bodies and slept-in clothes wafted through the air and, involuntarily, I drew back when the pungent odor penetrated into my nostrils. Pippa, I noticed, seemed to be indifferent and plowed straight into the mob. Naturally, all the talk centered on events in the homeland. The snatches I caught were in no way revelatory, sometimes repeating word for word conversations I had heard in Moscow.

In one corner stood the priest, still wearing his gold-embroidered vestments, gesticulating with elegantly shaped fingers ending in incongruously long and yellow fingernails, sporting long jet-black hair and an impressively gray beard that conspired to make him resemble a fanatical Old Believer, and pontificating in a deep bass about the war as God's punishment for the Russians' sinful ways. "Mortal sin always calls forth God's wrath," the *batyushka* thundered, as the fearful babushkas rubbed their hands and looked up at him tearfully. "Repent, I say to thee, repent, and salvation shall be yours."

Through no fault of my own, his eyes locked into mine. "*Molodoi chelovek*, you look skeptical, young man. Are you a sinner?" Struck dumb momentarily by the unexpected accusation, I said nothing and, instead, tried to produce a disarming smile that probably struck him as a silly and defiant grin. "You *are* a sinner!" he shouted, his finger waving at me like a sword. After I mumbled something in my defense, he appeared to have a vision and, after lowering his gaze from the heavens, resumed his jeremiad: "And a corrupt foreigner, too! And you dare come to my church and flaunt your fancy clothes before my flock. Away with ye!" He spat on the ground, missing my shoe by a few inches. "Away!" The old ladies in the flock glared at me, punched their fists in the air, stomped their feet, and bleated, "*shpion, etot amerikanets shpion.*"

Being denounced by a crazy cleric as a sinner was bad enough, but being accused by some crazed ladies of being an American spy was infinitely worse, so I lowered my head in a semblance of remorse, took three hesitant steps backward, and, grabbing Pippa by the arm, led her out of the crowded square and toward the sea.

"What did I do to deserve *that*?" I felt angry and humiliated and more than slightly worried that the incident portended a disastrous stay in Nice.

"They almost stoned you," she laughed. "Would've served you right, ducky. The look on your face was—still is—one of complete disbelief. That priest knows faces and what they hide and yours was obviously hiding all manner of illicit thoughts." She poked me in the ribs. "And, besides, you do look like a perfectly untrustworthy American with nothing but subversively anti-Russian thoughts on his mind. Why, anyone can see that."

"Just take me to that bistro," I growled, but not before assuming a look of what I hoped would pass for immaculate innocence. "I need a drink—and I don't mean wine."

The meal was in fact quite decent—she had a seafood pizza, I went for the grilled sardines and *Salade Niçoise*—and, after our espresso cups were emptied, we paid the *garçon* and headed for the promenade. The cloudless sky was almost white with sunlight and the sea was quite still, resembling a sheet of slightly undulating aluminum foil. The gulls circled overhead, their predictably mournful cries punctuating the buzz produced by the intermingled conversations and hawkers' yells.

Couples paraded up and down, many dressed in Sunday finery, with the women sporting flowing silk scarves and sleeveless dresses and the men opting for sunglasses and linen suits. The normalcy was almost shocking and the contrast with Russia, even with Tallinn and Minsk, couldn't have been greater. Here, life was just life. It went on in its recognizable patterns, to everyone's seeming satisfaction. We hadn't spoken since leaving the bistro and, with a pleasant languor settling over us, we remained and were happy to remain silent. At one point, Pippa interlocked her arm in mine, as if it were the most natural and most obvious thing in the world. I can't say I was thrilled—the alarm bells had begun ringing faintly—but the atmosphere was far too pleasant for me to resist.

We strolled all the way to the old town where we made a left and sauntered along the crooked streets, lost our bearings, entered several beautiful churches, and topped our adventures with overpriced crêpes and coffee in a spacious outdoor café. Displaying the advantages of her upbringing and education, Pippa accompanied our wanderings with a monologue about the various architectural styles of the churches, interspersed with slyly sardonic comments about a variety of Niçoise peccadillos we encountered along the way. Never having paid too much attention to the nuances that distinguished Baroque from Rococo and other styles—I could, however, deliver long-winded disquisitions on the Parthenon or the Roman Forum at the drop of a hat—I asked pointed questions, not out of politeness, but because she had really piqued my curiosity. I realized, after we had taken a table in some café, that she might have misinterpreted my queries and attentiveness as betokening romantic interest. To tell the truth, there was some, but only a bit, still not enough to overpower my better judgment and self-restraint. At least not yet.

We came back to the hotel by taxi and retired to our rooms, having agreed to meet at nine and continue our meanderings. "Let's top things off with the casino at the Hotel Negresco," she suggested. "The city's *beau monde* should be there in full force. It might be amusing."

"And expensive." I had become very conscious of my dwindling resources and the fact that I no longer had much of an expense account.

"Don't be a Scrooge, ducky. You only live once, after all."

*

The Negresco was lit up like the Christmas tree at Rockefeller Center. The temperature was mild, a slight breeze blew in from the ebony sea, and the leaden water rippled soothingly against the stones and reflected a distorted image of the hotel. Crowds of locals and tourists, the latter, both men and women, mostly Americans in running shoes, windbreakers, and baseball caps, thronged the Promenade des Anglais. The smartly attired usher opened the gilded door with a critical glance that signaled disapproval of our clothes—my standard-issue charcoal gray suit, unpressed white shirt, and red polyester tie and Pippa's strapless navy-blue cocktail party dress. I sported no Rolex and expensive jewelry was conspicuously absent from her ears, neck, wrists, and fingers. We strode in with what we hoped would pass for arrogant self-confidence and then, after following a party of four dressed in tuxedos and swishing gowns, found ourselves in the midst of the brightly lit, glittering casino.

"I feel like we're in a James Bond movie," I stated. "You know, I've been to Vegas and Atlantic City, but this"—I produced a slight whistle—"well, this is definitely a few cuts above my usual low standards."

"As I said, love, you only live twice." She looked around inquisitively. "Let's get some chips and play. How much money can you spare?"

I opened by exceedingly slim wallet, poked around inside, and informed her that I had "a hundred. Euros. Although, if we lose, it'll be rice and beans for the remainder of our trip."

"And I've got a hundred, too. Well, we won't be high rollers, but at least we won't embarrass ourselves."

"Too much, you mean," I grinned. "Did you notice how the usher looked at us with utter contempt?" She smiled, but ignored my question.

"Can you play any of these games—Blackjack, Bridge, Poker?"

"Not a clue, my dear. Think of me as the anti-Bond. Can you?"

She shook her head and frowned, as if I had greatly disappointed her. "Baccarat is too clever for us and obviously out of the question," she said, her voice rising inquiringly, in one final attempt to coax some flair out of me.

"Completely, totally, and absolutely out of the question. I can't even spell the word. Two c's or two r's?"

"Don't all you Yale boys play Poker and smoke cigars and drink whiskey?" she asked sweetly. "After a game of golf at the country club?"

"Never cared for them. Or for golf. A silly game with grown men with distended bellies taking turns trying to whack a tiny ball. Chess, on the other hand, now that's—"

"Boring," she pronounced *ex cathedra*.

"Where are the slot machines? I think we can manage those."

"Too jejune, ducky. And," while jabbing me in the ribs with a sharp elbow, "need I remind you, too American."

"Then I guess it's the roulette table for us. I think we can figure that out. It's black or red or—"

"—odd or even." After scratching her heavily powdered nose, she cautiously added, "I think."

We broke into laughter. She took my arm and led me toward the roulette table. The throng that surrounded it appeared to consist of as many casually dressed tourists as elegantly attired French, presumably because they, the tourists, had, like us, figured that roulette would be least intimidating. We inched our way forward. "You play the rich dame and place the bets," I suggested, "and I'll be the gigolo and stand behind you, like in the movies." That seemed more appropriate for these monied surroundings. Besides, I found the movement of the ball, the whir of the wheel, and the dignified silence of the croupier to be mesmerizing and wanted to savor the luxury of watching without thinking.

Pippa placed a chip on red and won. Then on even and she lost. Then on black (victory), followed by odd (defeat). And so it went for about half an hour. The pile of chips rose and fell and rose and fell like a seesaw. She was frustrated by the lack of progress, while I was delighted that, if the trend continued, I'd come away with my pocket book intact and my shirt on my back. Then, amazingly, luck smiled on her and she won big and, after the dealer finished pushing some chips in our direction, I noticed that she doubled the amount we had started with.

A scantily clad waitress passed by with champagne, so I took two flutes and, handing one to Pippa, implored, "Maybe we should stop? Or at least put two hundred aside?"

"Don't be such a bloody bore, Steven," she scolded. "I've only just warmed up." Then she said conspiratorially, "Take a look at that spanking chap over there." She tilted her head slightly to the left. "The bald fellow with an eye patch, mustache, and goatee. Whom does he remind you of?" Her eyes were twinkling maliciously.

He was a character straight out of a Bond film, wearing an expensive tuxedo and sporting a red carnation pinned to his lapel. I almost burst out laughing, but she squeezed my arm and placed one finger on her lips.

"What's the name of that quintessential Bond villain?"

I proceeded to answer my own question. "Le Chiffre, Blofeld, Goldfinger… Is that who you had in mind?"

"No, silly," she squeezed my arm harder. "Take a close look, a really, really close look."

I did and still had no clue. "I give up. Who?"

"Why Pitun, of course! He could be his *Double-gänger*."

"His what?" I knew what she had in mind, but decided to play hard to get.

"His *Double-gänger*," she said impatiently, "his twin."

"Oh, you mean his *Doppelgänger*!" I corrected her with unconcealed relish and was immediately rewarded for my better knowledge of German with a swift dig in the abdomen.

"Just look!"

I did, more closely this time, and had to agree. The ridiculous eye patch, mustache, and goatee got in the way, but, if you erased them in your mind's eye, then the guy really did look like Pitun. Most telling were his eyes—deeply set, beady, and cold and resembling those of a dead fish.

"Wouldn't it be a pip if he really *were* Pitun? We'd have the scoop of the century."

"And," the cautious side in me chimed in, "possibly risk getting killed. The man's a fugitive. Half the people at this table are probably his bodyguards and assassins. Assuming, of course, that this really *is* Pitun and not just a bit of delusional daydreaming on our part."

"Well," she concluded, "there's only one way to find out." Uh-oh, I thought, when Pippa set her mind on some harebrained scheme, it was time to head for the hills.

She pulled me toward the table, admonished me not to make any crazy bets, and began sliding toward the Russian dictator's look-alike. I tried to grab her, but she eluded my lunge and, with a naughty smile gracing her lips, positioned herself next to the man. She studiously avoided my glances except once, when she winked. Fortunately, the *Doppelgänger* was oblivious of her presence and focused all his attention on the clicking wheel. He was, I surmised from the dwindling pile of chips, losing, perhaps even losing badly. The chips he had were evidently of a higher order of magnitude than ours. He wasn't playing with two hundred euros, but with thousands—without losing his cool. Another reason to suspect he might be the real deal?

Thirty minutes later and his chips all gone, the man rose from his seat, turned on his heels, appeared to mumble his apologies to the people behind him, and, squeezing through, left the table. Pippa rejoined me and averred, "The plot thickens, love, the plot thickens." She collected the chips and we moved away.

"Don't tell me it's really him?" I was, frankly, incredulous.

"Could be, love, could be. He's the right height, about five feet six, like me. I heard him mutter a curse under his breath and it sounded Russian—something like chortoo."

"*K chertu*," I corrected her. "It means, literally, to the devil. Russians say it all the time, especially to express anger or frustration."

"Which probably means that he's—"

"—Russian."

"Exactly.

"So, if it walks like a duck and talks like a duck?"

"Exactly," she beamed triumphantly.

"A good deduction, Watson, a perfectly reasonable deduction, but, alas, no dice. Not yet, in any case. We lack conclusive evidence. Thus far, it's all suppositions, mere conjectures based on a little pile of circumstantial evidence. Did you consider," my voice had dropped to a whisper, "that it really could be a

Doppelgänger? Hell, why not? Stranger things have been known to happen. Besides, neither of us has ever met the real Pitun. We're comparing this man's physical features with those we've seen in two-dimensional photographs or on television. That could be apples and oranges."

"Or he might be the genuine article," she surmised. "And if he is—" she paused for me to complete the sentence.

"—this could be a gold mine."

"Exactly, ducky."

"There's only one way to find out," I repeated her conjecture of a few minutes ago, "and that's to come back tomorrow and follow him when he leaves."

"Oh, how delicious!" she swooned. "It'll be just like *From Russia with Love* and I can be the delicious Tatyana!"

"Right," I replied with rather less enthusiasm, "but don't forget the deadly Rosa Klebb with that poison-spike shoe of hers."

Outside, the crowds hadn't thinned, the sea still rustled like leaves in autumn, and the palm trees lining the promenade still stood guard over the merrymakers. Pippa took my arm again and we walked in silence back to the hotel. The empty streets were a pleasant complement to the refreshingly cool air and the tranquility was interrupted only by the incidental clicking of heels or the muted barking of dogs.

"This could be dangerous," I said after we had entered the lobby. "If he is who we think he might be, he'll resent our intrusion. And if he's not, he might be some arms dealer or drug lord or pimp. Are you sure we want to do this?"

"Let's sleep on it," she said conciliatorily. But then, before we alighted the lift, "Do we really have a choice?"

"No," I said, "no, I suppose not."

We kissed on the cheek before she exited. Both of us had

displayed admirable self-restraint, especially in light of the romantic surroundings and the potential intrigue. I slept well that night, though in the morning, just before awakening, I dreamt of Pitun and his twin. They were dressed as carnival hucksters selling snake oil or some such concoction. The setting, though accurate, was benign, but I awoke with a shudder anyway.

*

Next day, Pippa and I played the tourists. She showed me Herzen's grave, atop which stood a statue of the great Russian liberal; we visited the Matisse villa and admired his sculptures and cut-outs; we strolled through the contemporary art museum, where Pippa explained why Yves Klein's purple was so magnificent (I wasn't fully convinced). Both of us were less than impressed by Niki de Saint-Phalle's multicolored sculptures. Afterwards, we had a wonderful bouillabaisse in the old port, where the menus were still mostly in French and few tourists dared roam without guides or maps. We walked back to the hotel along the promenade, but not before a quick detour in the old town for an espresso and a subsequent interlude on the beach. The pervasiveness of potential romance was overwhelming, even for an old cynic like me, but our self-discipline continued to be commendable.

At one point, hoping to break the palpable tension, the unexpressed expectation of something that should not happen, I purposefully reached for the absurd and asked her point blank why she insisted on using *ducky* so often. Was it an affectation? A joke? No, she answered, she had served as a waitress in an East End pub for a summer—The Blind Beggar: Had I heard of it? It was where one of the notorious Kray brothers had shot "some bugger" in 1966—and picked it up from the working-class clientele, initially as a way of fitting in, then as a figure of speech that reminded her of a good time in her life. I countered with my experience as a waiter at Pepe's, a pizza joint in New Haven that was especially popular with the Yale crowd. Unfortunately, I had only learned to curse in Italian. We both laughed.

That evening, we found the twin in the same place at the roulette table. So as to maintain some anonymity, we decided against joining him; instead, I wandered about looking bored, in the hope of espying his bodyguards or other suspicious characters, while Pippa set herself in an easy chair half-hidden by a palm tree near the entrance, whence she could observe who came and went. We felt very professional: my CIA forefathers would have been proud of their amateur spy.

Like the day before, the twin finished playing—he appeared to have lost all his chips again: clearly, he was a man with money to burn and no aversion to temporary defeat—just before midnight and left. I followed him at a safe distance, fully expecting a cloak-and-dagger chase through the city's dark streets to ensue, but, instead, he made for the reception desk, exchanged a few words with a bespectacled platinum blonde, and, waving good-bye, stepped into the elevator, and disappeared.

"Well, at least we know where he's staying," I said with disappointment. "What now?"

"Don't be a dunderhead," she replied and sailed toward the reception and, turning on all her feminine charms, began flirting with the middle-aged man in a maroon jacket and canary-yellow bow-tie who serviced the telephone. Vigorous nods and broad smiles followed and a few minutes later Pippa was motioning to me to join her at the bar. We ordered martinis —"shaken, not stirred," she insisted—and she explained her flirtatious behavior and its not unexpected results.

"If you ask nicely, the hotel personnel—"

"You mean the men."

"—the *male* hotel personnel will always tell you what you want to know."

"You mean, tell *you*." I ignored her scowl and said, "And that is what?"

"The twin checked in three days ago. He has a German passport, goes by the name of Woldemar Peters, has no French, and speaks English with a thick Slavic accent. Oh, and he spends an hour every morning in the fitness room." As she finished speaking, a grin had supplanted the scowl.

"Woldemar is an obvious variant of Vladimir," I pointed out, "and Peters—as in Petersburg, where Pitun was born? And he does like to work out. Could be our man."

"Could be, indeed." She daintily fished out one of the olives and popped it into her mouth. "If you think about it, coming to Nice makes sense. First, there's a sizable Russian community here, many of whom are probably his supporters. Second"—by now, she was counting off the points on the fingers of her left hand—"he's reputedly stolen some seventy-eighty billion dollars. The Riviera real estate would be a natural place to park his cash. Third," she smiled embarrassedly, "third I forgot."

"And third," I finished her thought, "Nice is easy to reach and easy to escape from, should the need arise."

"Exactly," she cried. "And fourth, if you're going to leave your country and hide out, it may as well be in one of the loveliest spots in the world."

"Bingo."

"So, tomorrow morning we come here for breakfast. We observe the venerable Monsieur *Double-gänger*"—she emphasized all four syllables in a transparent show of defiance—"and try to follow him. And, if all works out as planned, we accost him in some public place and get an interview."

"It won't be that easy, you know. Murphy's Law will assert itself—it always does—and don't forget that he's a killer, probably surrounded by killers."

"That's why I have a big, strong, resourceful, and clever man like you to protect me, James."

"Let's just hope we don't only live once, Tatyana." I pronounced the name in Russian, with the *tya* forming one syllable and the emphasis on it.

"That's Ta-ty-a-na to you, ducky," she corrected me, emphasizing the third syllable. "This Bond bird is pure-bred English."

*

Figuring that the twin would need an hour and a half for his workout and shower, we estimated that we needn't show up earlier than seven-thirty. Besides, the breakfast room opened at seven, so, even if he arrived then, we'd still be in time to catch him. Our calculations were correct. The elegantly attired dining room was still sparsely populated and we were able to take a window table that offered a clear view of the entire space while enjoying some seclusion. The obsequious waiter, a short man with an artificial smile pasted to his chubby face, brought us two leather-bound, gold-embossed menus and enquired whether we would like coffee or tea or something else. We ordered two double espressos and surveyed the offerings.

"Good heavens!" I almost gagged upon seeing the prices. "A cup of coffee costs ten euros. And just look at the other prices! A boiled egg—one measly boiled egg: *fifteen* euros. Two scrambled eggs: *twenty*. And look here: a measly croissant costs *twelve*." I shut the menu and grumbled, "It's toast for me. Today and for the rest of the week."

Pippa cast me a *faux*-innocent glance that might have been intended to soften the sarcasm that followed. "What were you expecting, Steven—a breakfast buffet with all-you-can-eat waffles?"

"No, no, not that," I hesitated, "but *fifteen* dollars for a coffee?"

"Ç'est la vie," she stated with a smirk.

I would have responded and our tussle would have needlessly continued, had the twin and three muscular men who must have been his bodyguards stepped inside and lumbered toward a table some five yards from us—a bit too close for comfort, as far as I was concerned, but there was nothing we could do about it, so I said nothing. The twin snapped his fingers and three waiters, all carbon copies of ours, instantly appeared with four plates of scrambled eggs and buttered toast, a jar of what could have been pickled herring, a large pot of coffee, and a basket of breads and pastries. The twin obviously had clout. Silently, the four men threw themselves on the food, dispensing with knives and using the bread to mop up the grease. Just as obviously, the twin and his colleagues had no class.

"Look at how they're eating," Pippa sneered. "Worse than you Americans. They can only be Russians."

When they had finished, they extracted cigars and cigarettes from their inside jacket pockets and leaned back to enjoy them. The restaurant forbade smoking, of course, but no one dared remind them of their transgressions. Yes, they had clout —as well as big fists and, if the bulges were what I thought they were, barely concealed guns. The other guests glared at them disapprovingly, but the four carried on as if they owned the hotel, which, come to think of it, was not as crazy a possibility as it sounded.

A few minutes later, a Frenchman—I could tell by his nattily trimmed mustache and beard and tasseled shoes and fashionable designer suit—popped in, surveyed the tables, and tiptoed toward their table. "*Bon jour*," he purred, clicking his heels smartly. "Bonn dzhoorr," said the twin, while his entourage just nodded and made room for the newcomer. They then switched to broken English. Thanks to the surrounding hubbub and their lowered voices, Pippa and I could only make out snatches of their conversation. I distinctly heard the words Russia, money, and power, but they amounted to nothing. Then the Frenchman cried, "voila!" and extended his hand; the twin grabbed it and, with both men grinning, the Frenchman bade the group "*au revoir*"—to which the twin replied "ow rrevoyer," while his colleagues only grunted—and, clicking his heels again, departed.

"The Frog is probably military," Pippa observed. "No one except for officers clicks heels anymore, not even we Brits."

"Suspicious?"

"Not necessarily. He could be a friend. Or a casino chum."

"Or he could be a rogue French general teaming up with Pitun to launch a counterattack in Russia."

Pippa rolled her eyes. "Now, you're letting your over-wrought imagination carry you away. Let's eliminate the banal possibilities first before we jump to outlandish conclusions. Fair enough, Steven?" She was smiling again as she finished speaking and I had no choice but to answer, "sure." In any case, the four men had risen from the table and were heading for the door. As much as it pained me, I dropped twenty-five euros on the table and rushed out after them. The twin made a left at the corner and headed away from the sea. His three companions followed about three yards behind him. Ten yards behind them, we made up the rear, arm in arm, pretending to be the couple we were not.

*

The twin clearly knew where he was going. Just before we reached the train station, he scooted down a small staircase and headed for a tunnel. The pathway was narrow, but the din from the traffic served as an excellent distraction, and, although we fell back a few more yards, we emerged from the tunnel un-detected. The neighborhood had suddenly changed. This was, literally, the other side of the tracks and all the signs, sounds, and faces were Middle Eastern. The twin marched ahead for half a block and then, after pausing briefly before a dilapidated building covered with Arabic graffiti, he darted inside. His three companions parked themselves near the entrance, while we adroitly made a right and disappeared, still arm in arm, down the street. The sun had risen and shone into our eyes and, I hoped, had succeeded in blinding the twin's bodyguards as well.

"Well, so much for today." I confess to having been relieved by what appeared to be a quick termination of our cloak-and-dagger misadventure.

"Don't be so quick to surrender, Steven," Pippa replied. "We'll have a coffee"—and she pulled me into a Middle Eastern café full of bearded men with worry beads, shapely tea glasses, and backgammon boards—"and wait for them to leave. At the least we might be able to find out whom he visited in this unlikely neighborhood."

The waiter pointedly ignored her, so I ordered two Arabian coffees. The price was all of two euros. "Now *that*," I beamed, "is rather more my style." Pippa just shook her head and mumbled, "You're incorrigible, Steven, even for a bloody Yank."

Possibly unnerved by the abrupt cessation of the clicking of dice—I was certainly unnerved—Pippa fondled the cup but left the coffee untouched and, rising to her feet every few minutes, slid past the stares and, poking her head through the doorway, glanced outside; after the fifth or sixth time, she whispered that "The coast is clear" and downed the coffee in one swift motion. "Can't let good money go to waste, ducky, now can we?" she said and we exited as inconspicuously as possible. The place erupted in guffaws as we shut the door.

"And they say we're the Orientalists," she said with a huff. "Some irony, ducky." I didn't get the reference and, and after mumbling a noncommittal uh-huh, grabbed her elbow and steered us left. "I think you were heading in the wrong direction," I explained and this time she responded with an equally noncommittal uh-huh. Fortunately, we had no time to continue this scintillating exchange and, as we approached the house and were ready to cross the street, we looked in both directions and saw the twin and his friends heading back for the tunnel.

"Oh, what luck!" Pippa squealed, her equanimity restored. "I'll reconnoiter the house, while you follow them. We'll meet back at the hotel later in the afternoon." I hesitated, but she continued, "Don't worry about me, Steven. I'll be fine."

I didn't tell her that I wasn't worrying about her. I was worrying about *myself*. I didn't fancy getting beaten up or worse just for the sake of a juicy story. My days as a derring-do foreign correspondent had long since ended. Pippa, being younger, had not yet developed those qualms and reservations. Well, I'd stay back, way back, and see. The whole thing might, with any luck, turn out to be a wild-goose chase.

The geese retraced their steps and then, a few blocks before reaching the promenade, made a right. A few minutes later and I could see the gleaming onion domes of the Orthodox church Pippa and I had already visited. Two burly men in track suits and running shoes were loitering in the square and, as the twin exchanged three kisses with both and heartily embraced them, the bodyguards drifted off into the shade, while I strode resolutely toward the church and, crossing myself ostentatiously, entered its cool and welcoming darkness, while hoping and praying that the oversized priest with a yen for expectorating on American spies would not be there to greet me.

Fortunately, the Orthodox have no pews, so I was able to position myself next to an icon of St. George spearing a dragon and could, while continuing with my *faux* genuflections, see the threesome out of the corner of my right eye. Ten minutes later, they embraced again and the twin rejoined his guards. I completed my devotions with one more genuflection and, after stepping into the glare of the increasingly hot sun, decided to follow the mysterious duo. Come what may, I had learned one important thing: the twin was definitely Russian and he obviously had intimate friends in Nice.

The two men had no reason to think I was on their heels, so they sauntered casually for a few blocks until they reached a non-descript, beige-colored building with dirty windows and dull green shutters and, after unlocking the heavy door with their own key, shuffled inside. I waited a few minutes and then approached the building. A metal sign, in Russian and French, declared from beneath the obscenities scrawled upon it that this was the headquarters of the *Union des patriotes russes*. Having written several stories a few years ago about the resurgence of right-wing extremism in Russia, I knew of them by their Russian name—*Soiuz russkikh patriotov*, or the SRP. It was a far-right organization that traced its lineage to the *Narodno-Trudovoi Soiuz* (or the People's Labor Alliance), a fascistoid émigré group that had opposed Soviet rule, but supported a resurgent Russia.

The SRP was little different in its political leanings and had, unsurprisingly, supported the Pitun regime unconditionally for the duration of its existence. They didn't like everything Pitun said or did—they criticized him for being *too* moderate—but they fully subscribed to his vision of an authoritarian and imperial Russia that deserved to flex its muscles. I had no doubt that they viewed ongoing events in the homeland with panic, alarm, and disgust. If any grouping could be expected to try to reverse the tide of history, it was the SRP. I didn't know how many members and resources they had. All these frustrated émigrés exaggerated their influence and importance and implied that the whole country supported them. More likely than not, they could count on several hundred men and women—interestingly, I had learned that women were as prone to be fanatical Russian extremists as men, both now as well as throughout Russian history—in Europe and another several hundred in Russia. But numbers didn't matter as much as who they were. The SRP claimed to have its people in the upper ranks of the *siloviki*—the forces of coercion that served as Pitun's power base—which was not implausible. After all, who else but the men with guns would be most drawn to the SRP's brand of kooky extremism? If Pitun were planning a Napoleonic comeback, then the SRP would be indispensable.

Back in the hotel, I knocked on Pippa's door. She opened it, with a drink in one hand and a broad smile on her face. "I have great news," she bragged. "So do I," I countered, "but you first."

She had examined the residents of the building and one of them was a man by the name of Vladislav Nikoforoff. The name meant nothing to me, so Pippa explained that Nikoforoff, who had left Russia in disgust at Gorbachev's liberalizing reforms, was one of the Nice Russian community's richest men. He had bought the dump he lives in many years ago and refused to move when the area lost its French character. A man like him, Pippa continued, would be sure to back a reptile like Pitun, who probably went there to pay his respects and discuss his plans. My turn came and I informed Pippa of the assignation in front of the church and my subsequent discovery of the SRP building.

"Verily," she summed up, "the plot thickens. We know he looks like Pitun, we know he's got a fat wallet, we know he's Russian, and we know he has dealings with Russian fascists." Her face brightened suddenly. "Oh, and we know one more thing. Lord, I almost forgot. That Frenchman at breakfast: do you know who he is?" My face was blank. "I flirted with that little receptionist again—the man thinks I'm quite fetching, by the way —and, lo and behold, he told me he's Jean Rougement, one of the leading apparatchiks in the local branch of the Le Pen party, the *Rassemblement national*. Want to guess around whom the nation hopes to rally?"

"He's our man, then," I whispered. I had suddenly become quite fearful, as the reality of what we were doing—stalking a bloodthirsty dictator who was planning a revanche—struck me with full force. "Pippa, do we know what we're up to? This could turn out," I hesitated for a second, uncertain of how to complete the sentence, "well, badly—for us, I mean—*very, very* badly."

"It's too late to back out, ducky. Oh," she said with as casual a tone as she could muster, "there's one tiny little thing I forgot to tell you."

"What?" I expected it to be some minor detail. Instead, Pippa produced a shocker.

"They saw me. Don't look so surprised, Steven. I ran into the twin and his chaps near the Negresco—quite by accident, mind you, just after I had finished my enquiries regarding Rougemont. All of a sudden, there they were, which surprised me, even though it shouldn't have, since they reside there. Sorry, I'm becoming incoherent." She took a deep breath. "Anyway, they saw me and one of the thugs stared me in the eyes. I batted my eyelashes and said something in French, but I think they know we've been on their tail."

"But they could've thought you're just some crazy lady," I said hopefully.

"Possibly. All I know is that he looked at me, and not just casually, but for a few seconds. He didn't just see me, Steven. He actually *looked* at me. Now, what that means I don't know, though I do know I didn't quite fancy his doing so. Perhaps he thought he was flirting. Perhaps he was in a bad mood. Or perhaps he saw that you and I had been following them and wanted to signal to me—to us—that we should desist. Who knows? Anyway, we need to assume the worst." She screwed her eyes and pursed her lips in a most unattractive manner. "We've gone this far and it would be a shame to stop. I say we may as well see this to the end."

"Don't say the end," I pleaded. "Just say we need to take this further." Her forced smile didn't alleviate my anxiety. "But I suppose you're right," I concluded reluctantly.

Possibly hoping to lift my obviously dampened spirits, Pippa suggested that we "stay clear of the casino tonight. I'm not sure it would be wise to push our luck." That helped, but only a bit.

"And breakfast tomorrow?" My voice trembled slightly, as I knew what she would say.

"Sure—why not? It's not every day I get to drink ten-euro coffees."

I groaned, she pushed me out the door, and we agreed to meet in the lobby at seven. I slept badly, of course. Images of the twin and his thuggish colleagues swirled chaotically in my head and I kept analyzing Pippa's encounter with the bodyguard and trying to concoct convincing alternative explanations for his threatening behavior. In Moscow, death had been all around me, but seemed to affect only others. Being an observer made the tension just bearable. Here, the threat was infinitely smaller, but, inasmuch as it was directed at us, it felt—and obviously was—much more menacing.

*

Having abandoned all pretense of sleep just before dawn, I was first to appear in the lobby and decided to sit in one of the polished leather chairs and pretend to read *Nice Matin* or *Le Monde*. Despite my miserable French, I was able to make out the headlines: the chaos in Russia was continuing, sparked by additional bombings, assassinations, ambushes, ethnic cleansings, and full-scale offensives. The Baltic nations had apparently joined forces with the Poles to drive the Russians out of Kaliningrad. A map showed Ukrainian flags extending deep into the Kuban. A photograph of the Kremlin revealed that a few more bombs had destroyed parts of its walls. Some general by the name of Fedotov was depicted as snarling and pointing. The caption appeared to say something about his having a *force de frappe*—or nuclear weapons. In a word, Russia's collapse was continuing, possibly even accelerating. We were missing nothing by being here—especially compared to the discovery that we may have made.

The receptionist interrupted my cogitations by asking if I was Monsieur Steven Smith. Yes, I was, I said, and he handed me an envelope with my name and Pippa's scrawled across the front and the Hotel Negresco logo in the upper left-hand corner.

I put it to my nose, but it was not perfumed. Too bad: alas, I'd be having no clandestine liaisons with mysterious women clad in black. I bent it, but the inside was pliable and crackled like paper. My curiosity got the better of me and, without waiting for Pippa, I pulled back the flap and removed an off-white piece of hotel stationery. The text consisted of one line and a name: "Please be meeting me for breakfast today at 7:30. W. Peters." Never (or almost never) in my life had so pithy a statement had such an emotional impact on me. I shuddered, my heart beat rapidly, and a profoundly unpleasant nausea lodged itself in my gut.

"You look like you're having a heart attack," Pippa cheerfully observed. "What's the matter, ducky? Seen a ghost?"

"Just about," I mumbled and handed her the note. "The receptionist gave it to me a few minutes ago."

She read it quickly and cried, "But this is marvelous, Steven! He knows who we are and he wants to meet us. I wager that he wants to give us an interview. Why the white face? This is the best possible news, especially after the scare I had yesterday."

She was right, of course, perhaps not about the interview, but certainly about this being better than yesterday's development. On the other hand, when a dictator with a reputation for ordering hits on his political opponents knows who you are, complacency and composure aren't exactly called for.

Once again, she interrupted my soul-searching. "Well, let's go, Steven! We have twenty minutes to get there, ducky. A man like Pitun isn't accustomed to waiting for his underlings. Remember, he's even made heads of state wait for him." She seized my arm and pushed my enervated body through the revolving door. "On the double, we're about to have an encounter with history."

I wanted to say "or death," but decided to keep my mouth shut and not spoil her festive mood. The nausea, needless to say, hadn't subsided.

We arrived somewhat breathless at the Negresco at just before seven-thirty and were happy to see that there was no sign of Mister Peters in the breakfast room. But the ever-vigilant waiter, obsequiously asking us if we were his guests, directed us to a table set for three. An adjacent table, also set for three, had presumably been readied for the bodyguards. We sat down and, just as I realized that I was facing the glare of the window (I had heard enough spy stories from relatives to know that put one at a disadvantage), the twin appeared and, a broad smile of recognition decorating his ruddy face, grabbed our hands, slapped my back, and took a seat. The nausea had disappeared, replaced by an equally unpleasant combination of apprehensiveness and fear.

"Shall we speak Russian or English?" he asked.

"English, please," Pippa said. "My Russian is a tad rusty."

He smiled again and looked at me. "So, you are Meester Steven Smees"—and with that introduction he proceeded to relate every detail of my life story, including references to boat shoes and Polo shirts. Then, addressing Pippa, he repeated his performance, even noting her employment at the pub that made the Krays famous. The purpose of the show was obvious. He knew everything about us. Moreover, he still had the resources to know everything about us. In other words, he was still who he had been for decades in Russia. I don't know about Pippa—which he pronounced Pee-Pah—whose patrician demeanor always managed to hide her innermost feelings, but I was intimidated.

"So," she retorted drily, "you know exactly who we are." His eyes twinkled. "But, please do remember that we in turn know exactly who you are," and, after that bit of chutzpah, she mimicked his performance with an awe-inspiring cornucopia of details about his personal and professional life. Way to go, Pippa, I cried silently.

Peters-Pitun was visibly amused and, clapping delicately, almost effeminately, he cried, "Brava! Bravissima!" Then he snapped his fingers at one of the waiters lurking near a marble column and, almost immediately, a variety of mountainous dishes arrived, ranging from scrambled eggs to pickled herring to caviar, along with every possible pastry, roll, and bread. "Deeg een," he ordered and, following his example, we attacked the delicacies and soon left an empty field of battle. "Gud, yes?" he enquired. "Very," I said. "Uh-huh," Pippa, who had eaten far more than she was used to, grunted.

"You vant interview, yes?"

"Yes," we both chimed in.

His instructions were terse: "Tonight, seven times, my room. Nomber five-tree-seven." He nodded at his companions and the four of them bolted upright and left. Stunned by his performance—there was no other word for what had just transpired—Pippa and I turned to each other and exploded with laughter. "You vant interview, yes?" she said, her voice lowered and her hands mimicking claws. "I vant to dreenk your blood, yes?"

"Not so loud," I admonished, barely able to restrain my own giggles. "They might see or hear us."

She became serious for a second. "By the way, what in bloody hell is seven times?"

"It's a direct translation from the Russian. He means seven o'clock, of course. So, shall we take up Count Dracula on his offer?" Oddly enough, my anxiety had been put to rest by Pitun's exact knowledge of our biographies, his command of the situation, and his bravura performance, so, with my qualms more or less dissipated and my nerves more or less settled, my question was purely rhetorical.

"Vee shall be dere at seven times on ze dot!" Her demeanor again acquired a serious expression. "But, in the meantime, we have an entire day to kill, so I suggest we do some follow-up investigations of our own: Monsieur Rougement and—"

"—our good friends at the Union of Russian Patriots. Together or apart?"

"Together," she said firmly. "After yesterday, together. Pitun may be a killer, but he's also a charmer. His thugs, on the other hand, have none of his endearing qualities and I suspect that the chaps at the Union are no different."

*

It took us half an hour of casual strolling along the promenade to reach the building that housed the SRP. I rang the doorbell, a male voice asked in French who we were, Pippa answered, and a buzz ensued. We crossed a foul-smelling courtyard with a trash bin overflowing with bottles, eluded several motley cats, saw a rat sitting on a window ledge, sidestepped a greasy puddle, and climbed the creaking stairs to the third floor, where one of the burly men I had followed met us. He waved us inside and we found ourselves in an apartment-turned-office with book-lined walls, stacks of papers, opened and unopened cardboard boxes, old typewriters collecting dust on shelves, and a few computers, though mostly older models, gracing several of the desks. A thick layer of smoke hung over the rooms and all the ashtrays appeared to be full.

We followed him into an undersized office where he pointed to two uncomfortable-looking chairs, introduced himself with a slight bow as Ivan Ivanovich Stepankoff, and deposited himself into a comfortable-looking leather chair, immediately lighting a cigar. "Cuban," he pointed out. "You vant?" No, thank you, we both shook our heads.

"Khow can I khelp you?" he smiled sweetly, leaning over and spreading his hands like the Messiah.

Pippa explained who we were and where we had just been in Russia, what we had seen and what we were told to expect by the Russians we met. Did he have any notion of where the president was? Had he abandoned his country? What would happen next? And how did the *Union des patriotes russes* hope to help the Motherland in her moment of dire need?

He leaned back, ran his hand through his non-existent hair, produced a deep frown that distorted his colossal eyebrows and concealed his eyes, snickered, and opined that the president was alive and well somewhere in Europe, that he had not abandoned his country or would ever abandon his country, that Russia was in the throes of a time of troubles, but would, as it always did in the past, rise again, and that the Union would, together with the president and all Russian patriots, both in Russia and in the emigration, ride into the Kremlin (whether on horses or on tanks he didn't say), holding high the triumphant banner of the victorious Saint George.

"Vee veel slay ze dragon. Ze Mongols cannot defeat Mozer Russia."

"And what exactly will the Union do?"

"Vee have brains," Stepankoff alleged in what struck me as a slight exaggeration, "and vee have mus-kles."

"Guns?"

"Per-khaps." And then he invoked the Bible and said something about an eye for an eye and a "toot for a toot." At that he flashed an incongruously full set of lily-white teeth, testimony, I decided, to regular dental cleanings—a behavioral trait that his ideological forerunner, the real *duce*, would probably have approved of.

"Is there anything you would like to tell the world?" Pippa enquired. "Anything at all?"

"Russia eez eeteernal," he said with finality, rose from his seat, asked if we would like a refreshment, and led us through the book-lined labyrinth to the exit. "Come aneetime," he smiled. "*Au revoir.*"

We repaired to a café a few blocks away and, sipping our espressos, compared mental notes. "What an oily character," Pippa shuddered. "He gives me the jitters. I wonder what Pitun sees in him—in them. They're just a bunch of washed-up émigrés. Lord, did you see those typewriters? And he expects to lead a victorious charge into Moscow—with Underwoods, no less!"

"That's his dream. The reality is, I think, that the SRP can probably provide Pitun with a few men with a claim to some historical legitimacy. If he hopes to make a triumphant return, he'll need an entourage of ex-statesmen and generals, and not just thugs. The SRP probably has a score of former ministers in its ranks—possibly with money." Then another thought occurred to me. "And I bet the SRP has ties to some Western intelligence services—the French almost certainly, and maybe the Germans and the Brits. That could be useful, particularly if push comes to shove and Pitun needs to be recognized as Russia's rightful president."

It was a little after eleven and Rougement would probably be having lunch in an hour. If we reached his office in time, we might even be able to join him—at his expense, of course. I paid the check, while Pippa ran out and hailed a cab. A threatening storm cloud had suddenly appeared overhead and, as it began to drizzle, the taxi sped along the glistening streets and dropped us off amid the pink buildings on the Place Massena. The rain had stopped, the sky was blue again, and the asphalt shimmered as pedestrians cast distorted shadows on the mirror-like puddles reflecting the sun. The crowds emerged from beneath the awnings and resumed their strolls and window-shopping. The offices of the National Rally were easy to find—the entrance was festooned with red, white, and blue ribbons—and we pushed open a heavy oak door and found ourselves before a wide marble staircase and a small reception on the right.

"You do the talking," I suggested, "and do turn on all your feminine wiles with Rougement. He's French, after all."

"Scrofulous lecher," she snorted and poked me in the ribs.

*

Rougement was delighted to see us. Two famous journalists representing the best of the world press in his humble abode! He gushed. How could he help us? He asked in grammatically correct though slightly accented English. Would we like some literature about the National Rally? Its latest party program, perhaps? Its numbers were growing; a cabinet seat almost went to one of its leading lights. It was now the model of respectability, having junked the extremist views that had originally propelled it, and its founder, to success. And so on.

I expected him to be crestfallen by our enquiries regarding Pitun, but, instead, his face lit up and he proceeded, as if on cue, to relate his views on the ongoing catastrophe in Russia, the obligation of the West to do everything possible to stem this humanitarian disaster, deal with the flood of refugees, and reestablish law and order in a country that had always been and always would be an integral part of Europe. France, for its part, would do everything it could to extend a helping hand to the nation that gave human civilization such geniuses as Dostoevsky, Tolstoy, Pushkin, and Tchaikovsky. "We would be poorer —less human, dare I say—without the Russian soul, would we not?"

Pippa interrupted his peroration—I suspected he could have gone on with his rhetorical legerdemain for another hour —by stating that we had accidentally espied him with Pitun and that the two of them appeared to have discussed something of great importance. "His return to Russia?" she asked with evident hesitation, almost as if she didn't want to provoke him into a verbal retreat. Instead, he reverted momentarily to French and cried, "*Exactement!*" Where else, he thundered, but with his people, did a great leader like Napoleon or Pitun belong? "Leading the nation to recovery and law and order!"

"And your role in this?" Remarkably, Pippa didn't take

the bait and say something untoward about Pitun's Napoleon complex. I was impressed by her discipline and resolve.

His ebullience became subdued and he whispered guardedly. "This is off the record, please." We nodded. "We have connections in the government and president's office. There have been, er, conversations—important conversations with important personages. More," he smiled, "I cannot say. You understand, of course. Discretion is indispensable."

"Of course, it is, of course," I said with the puffed-up self-importance of someone who supposedly dealt with top-secret materials every day. "May we assume that these important conversations with important people concerned Pitun's eventual restoration in Russia?"

"I am not at liberty to confirm or deny your assumption, except to say that it is not outlandish."

"And that France would not be opposed?" Pippa added.

"France always supports human, national, and civil rights as well as the legitimacy of popularly elected democratic leaders."

I could have maintained that Pitun's democratic legitimacy was less than nil, but decided against principled obstreperousness and opted for greasy gratitude. After all, Rougement had confirmed what we had suspected and that was all that really mattered.

Pippa then switched on her charm and began speaking French—something about culture, the opera, and the "*beauté de la langue française.*" Like a peacock, Rougement visibly swelled with pride and proposed that we have some coffee. I looked at Pippa and she said *oui* and resumed the conversation. She was up to something, so I thumbed through the brochures he had given us and struggled with the party program. She made a remark, he produced a booming guffaw, they briefly embraced, and it was obvious that the two were getting along famously. A few more minutes of whispered banter followed and then Pippa stole a glance at her watch, muttered, "O-la-la," and, excusing herself hurriedly, ordered me to rise. A few handshakes and smiles later, we were escorted to the exit, where Rougement, waving, pleaded, "Please come anytime at all. I am always happy to meet with friends." Alas, I thought, there was to be no free lunch today.

"So, what was that all about?"

"While you were pretending to read, I was working, ducky. The National Rally is providing Pitun with three million euros. And the Élysée Palace and Quai d'Orsay support him wholeheartedly. His words, not mine."

Impressed, I whistled softly. "That's about four million dollars, not quite enough to save Russia, but more than enough to enable Putin to procure a white stallion and stage a triumphant return."

"And if the French support him, I wouldn't be surprised if the Germans do, too."

"But not the Brits and probably not the Americans."

"Definitely not the Brits and almost definitely not the Yanks. But that needn't worry our lad. All he needs is enough international support to make his comeback credible. After that, it's all up to him anyway. The French won't send troops to Russia. Neither will the Germans or anyone else, for that matter."

"He'll fail," I contended with a confidence that surprised me. I rarely made predictions, but, after seeing the carnage and chaos in Russia, I couldn't imagine a reversal to the status quo ante anytime soon—and certainly not with Pitun as head of state.

"Probably. But can you imagine how much damage he could do—to *everybody*?"

"He doesn't care."

"But the French should," she said bitterly.

"The French?" I couldn't keep from chortling. "You've got to be kidding. The French would sell their mothers for a *soupçon* of *raison d'état*. Hell, they're worse than the Germans." I pointed to a bistro that appeared to serve seafood. "Let's eat something. I'm suddenly famished. That heavy breakfast must have finally worn off and Monsieur Rougement proved less than generous in his hospitality." Hoping to bring some closure to this topic, I added, "And, yes, I do know the Americans aren't much better. We're just farther away."

CHAPTER FOUR

Milan, Zürich, and Nürnberg

We were too jumpy to consider retiring to the hotel, so we spent the remainder of the day sauntering about, drinking too much coffee, having an occasional crêpe or *pissaladière*, and making jocular observations about the French and their odd customs in the Grand Lyon, a beautiful, spacious, old café on the Avenue Jean Médecin that used to fit into its Belle Époque surroundings, but that now, encircled by anonymous, mundane department stores, stuck out like a prima ballerina at a gathering of certified public accountants. At six forty-five we were in the lobby of the Negresco. At six fifty-five, we requested that the reception buzz Pitun's room. At exactly "seven times," he welcomed us with an elaborate bow and a wide grin that suggested he knew that we knew this was all for show. Several platters topped with multicolored delicacies, ranging from the salty to the sweet, adorned the counter; a full bar stood on a cart. The bodyguards immediately filed out, but a tall thin man with spectacles, light blue shirt, striped red-and-brown tie, brown linen suit, and black wing-tipped shoes remained.

"Meester Voronov," Pitun said after we had introduced ourselves. "Translator. He is speaking perfect English. Not," Pitun adopted a pose of modesty, "like mine."

"No tape recorders, no phones, no notes," Voronov ordered. "Are those ground rules acceptable?" Of course, they were, we both said. Pitun would likely be more forthcoming, less guarded in the absence of such paraphernalia. Besides, both of us were seasoned reporters and had good memories. And with two of us, we could easily reconstruct the entire conversation.

"Then, please be seated."

We took the couch; Pitun sat to our left in a gold-embroidered easy chair with a two-headed eagle serving as a monogram, while Voronov, whose obligations didn't just involve translating, soundlessly placed the platters on the coffee table and poured us all large vodkas and then, cradling a crystal glass, sat to our right.

"Eat!" Pitun commanded and we did. I went for the blini with caviar and several *petits fours*; Pippa sliced off some camembert and grabbed a bunch of grapes. A toast to peace followed and Pitun immediately launched into his soliloquy, pausing every few sentences to enable the slightly breathless Voronov to catch up. Voronov's translation was, I noticed, excellent. He missed no nuances and always conveyed the exact gist of Pitun's rhetorical flourishes. Unfortunately, Pitun said nothing we hadn't heard before: Russia was in trouble, he had had to leave in order to rally his forces, but now he would be back and all would be well.

"This is," I stated, speaking in Russian, "1917 and you are Lenin." I said that because I could think of nothing else to say after he had finished his speech, but he appeared to like the comparison and beamed. And then, uncertain of what to say next, I joked, "Why don't you go back to St. Petersburg in a sealed train?"

Pitun fell silent for a moment—had my off-the-cuff comment insulted him?—and then his eyes gleamed brightly, his smile broadened from ear to ear, and he clapped his hands repeatedly, crying, "Eureka!"

"*What? What* eureka?" I asked uncertainly and looked to Pippa for help, but she sat impassively, immersed in her own thoughts or daydreams, munching on a piece of cheese.

Pitun couldn't restrain his enthusiasm and spoke in English. "Breelliant idea, Meester Smees! Breelliant idea! Vee shall do that, exactly as you say. *By train*, Voronov! *Poezdom!* Like great Leneen. I like this Smees! *By train, Voronov, by train!* Vee go by train, Voronov, vee go by train. Oh, such a breelliant idea!" Then he leaned toward us and, taking Pippa's hand and mine, added, "And you veell be coming with me. You veell be there when I come and you veell write heestorical account of my triumph.

"Meester and Meesuss Dzhon Reed!" he added triumphantly.

Personally, I wasn't all that sure I found the comparison with the American communist who witnessed the revolution in Russia and rather hyperbolically claimed that it "shook the world" all that flattering, while the thought of accompanying Pitun on a train ride through Europe was definitely less than appealing. On the other hand, we *would* have unrestricted access to the man for a few days and most journalists would kill for just a few minutes.

"You expect to shake the world in ten days, Mister President?" Pippa asked.

"Een less!" he cried and filled our glasses. "Vee leave tomorrow!" His tone brooked no dissent, so Pippa and I meekly nodded, not at all sure what we had gotten ourselves into, and were informed that someone would inform us tomorrow morning when our train departed.

The merriment went on until ten, at which time Pitun abruptly excused himself, saying it was late and that he never went to sleep later than ten-thirty, and ordered Voronov to drive us to our hotel. We demurred, to Voronov's evident delight, and, after saying *au revoir* to Russia's bloody dictator, made a dash for the promenade, descended the stairs to the pebbly beach, and sat there for a while, letting the pleasant breeze and flickering waves clear our heads and settle our nerves.

All I could do was whistle and say, "What an evening!"

"What a story," she murmured. "And just think, Steven: it'll be a foreign correspondent's dream. All that time with Pitun. We were hoping for an interview and, instead—"

"—we're getting into bed with him."

"This could mean a Pulitzer for us, you know."

"Or a one-night stand with a sadist."

"Well, at least we know he won't be killing us on that train."

"At least not immediately," I grumbled. "But the Russians might." As might, I thought, my good friend Andrus and every other self-respecting Estonian.

*

Our train consisted of five old-fashioned first-class cars that, as Voronov proudly explained, usually served to transport romantically inclined Americans and Brits with money to burn as part of the Orient Express tours organized by some Franco-Turkish company. Passengers crossed the continent in the height of elegance, were treated to expensive wines and gourmet foods, and enjoyed luxurious compartments with every possible contemporary amenity made to resemble a late nineteenth-century article. The cost was exorbitant, of course, but Voronov was able to get, as he put it, a "good deal," thanks in no small measure to the fact that "certain French officials" made a strategic intervention and convinced the company that national security was at stake. "Which, of course, it is," concluded Voronov. However he managed to pull it off—and I couldn't imagine massive bribes not having been paid—I had to admire his enterprising spirit and quick thinking.

Our section of the platform contained about fifteen expectant passengers and their designer luggage, among whom we recognized Rougement and the two Russians from the Union of Patriots. I imagined that Vladislav Nikoforoff, the reclusive millionaire, was probably here as well. The others were for the most part nattily attired men and women, mostly middle-aged or older, sporting fine suits, cashmere coats, silk dresses, and a plethora of oversized jewels and scarves. Since the decision to travel by train had been made late last evening, they had obviously been assembled with some haste. I imagined they were probably French and Russian aristos from Nice and its environs. One couple did stand out: two oversized Americans who probably got here this morning on their private jet.

Pitun had clearly decided to make his entrance in grand style. No grubby revolutionaries for the new Lenin, no filthy proles, no *hoi polloi*. Nothing but the best—if not the brightest—suited him. But that made perfect sense. Pitun had always drawn on Russia's economic, political, and social elites for support. The people he bamboozled and kept quiescent with bread and circuses. The elites, in contrast, had to be actively wooed, and what better way to woo them than to signal that the *ancien régime* would be restored in all its glory?

As the would-be chroniclers of Pitun's trek home, we were given a suite—two compartments equipped with beds, bars, writing tables, easy chairs, and sinks separated by a common bathroom with a shower stall (the curtain was of some diaphanous material)—in the car next to his, a sign of our status that would surely not go unnoticed by the other passengers. Propinquity to the Sun King had defined the hierarchical relationships of the French court. Nothing, clearly, had changed.

Everything was perfect. Except for one thing. To my annoyance, Voronov and one of his minions knocked on my door and explained that, since much of what would transpire on the train would be off the record, he was collecting all our cell phones. Surely, I didn't mind, did I? It was a question of glasnost and security and, besides, the phones would be returned upon the journey's completion. I asked, with evident ill temper, whether he'd be wanting our laptops as well, but Voronov slipped into one of his most obsequious smiles and assured me that laptops were quite all right, especially as Pippa and I were "world-famous" correspondents who had to take notes and send emails. But why take our phones while still permitting us to communicate via the Internet? To which he immediately responded that, well, cell phones enabled their users to speak spontaneously and, alas, sometimes unwisely, while emails demanded a bit more deliberation and circumspection. His elaborate explanation struck me as absurd, but, not wanting to rock the boat and knowing that resistance was futile, I surrendered my phone and took the receipt prepared by the factotum.

As soon as they departed, I knew I had to have a drink. To my delight, the bar contained several regular-sized bottles, Swarovski crystal glasses, and a variety of snacks. If I wanted more, so the little handwritten card informed me, a tug on a tasseled cord would immediately hail a waiter. All I wanted for the time being was a double malt scotch, so I poured myself half a glass and downed it in one swift motion. My nerves settled, I glanced around the compartment once again. The curtains were of velvet and the bed posts were of carved mahogany. A full-length beveled mirror attached to the bathroom door completed the lavish ensemble. Needless to say, all the materials were expensive, while the tightly-woven carpet was of genuine Turkish origin. Having brought little, I unpacked my things in a few minutes and, walking through the bathroom, knocked on Pippa's door.

"Come in, Steven."

She was sitting in her easy chair, perusing a glossy brochure. "It's our itinerary. Our chum Pitun has a good sense of history."

"Did they take your phone, too? I think it's an outrage, don't—"

"Of course," she shrugged. "Frankly, I'm glad to be rid of the bloody thing. So, calm down, ducky, and have another drink. Scotch?" I nodded. Then, handing me the brochure, she explained, "We first go to Zürich—"

"Where Lenin spent part of the war!" I cried. Suddenly, the cellphones didn't matter: we were on the way to a great adventure, an encounter with history. We were on the way to the Finland Station in St. Petersburg!

"—and then we head north through Germany, where—"

"But surely the Poles and the Balts won't let us through," I objected, almost miffed by their historical truculence and outrageous unwillingness to facilitate our journey.

"—where, as I was *about* to say," she spoke with a hint of impatience bordering on annoyance, "they'll place the train on a barge of some kind and ship the entire bloody thing—"

"To St. Petersburg!" My ill temper had vanished entirely.

"Not exactly Lenin's route," she pointed out, "but, given the circumstances, close enough."

"But notice the symbolism," I hastened to add. "Peter built the city as a window to the West. And now, Pitun, who surely fancies himself as Peter the Great and Lenin all in one, will crawl back to his benighted nation by the very window originally built by Peter. The Russians can't help see that and be impressed."

"Which means that we're likely to spend about three full days in this tub," she said gloomily. "I've never cared for trains—too slow. And even opulence doesn't compensate for their monotony. That incessant rhythm—"

"It's like a waltz," I pointed out, "just listen when we start moving."

"Well, it may remind you of the waltz and imperial Vienna, but to me it's just a background noise that's too insistent to be ignored." She snorted. "It's more like Chinese water torture."

"Well, the bar is well stocked," I reminded her, "and I'm

sure that Pitun and his friends will keep us occupied. Do top off my drink, will you? And don't forget we're here to work—get an interview or two, serve as chroniclers, create the master narrative that will determine future interpretations of the history we're experiencing first hand."

"And to some degree creating." She yawned. "Don't fret, Steven, I'm just being a bore. It's not the bloody train or the monotony or anything like that. I've been thinking too much and I'm still not sure why we're here and that worries me and, when I get worried, I become a bore." She leaned toward me. "Pitun's supposed to be a strategic thinker, a grandmaster at geopolitical chess. Is it really like him to have become enamored of us and suggested spontaneously that we join him on a bloody choo-choo to the *Götterdämmerung*? Could that Voronov character have really organized all this in a few hours?" The last question was accompanied by an intentional snort.

"Why not?" I declared. "These guys have money, they have pull. And if Pitun enjoys the support of Paris, then he also enjoys the support of Berlin. Hell, they wouldn't let him board a barge in Lübeck if that weren't the case." I realized I was enjoying my counter-attack. "Now, is he using us? Of course, he is. Why shouldn't he? We walked right up to him and pretty much volunteered our services as two of the world's top journalists. And now he's got us in his pocket. But," I quickly added, "*we* have him in *ours*. He expects us to write a panegyric or, in any case, a tale of his heroic campaign. But, if we stick to the facts, we'll also expose him for what he is."

"A bloody dictator."

"Not immediately, of course, or else he'll push us off a speeding train."

"Ouch."

"But as step two, once this is over, we'll have a prize-winning book and you'll be able to impress your Cambridge pals with a Pulitzer. That's what *you* said. Remember?" Pippa responded with another magnificent yawn, so, resolving to treat her seeming indifference as an affirmation of my argument, I continued with my rosy projections of our glorious future.

Where this exaggerated sense of self-confidence came from I didn't know. Although I had a sneaking suspicion that the scotch had some role to play in my sudden conversion to sunny optimism, I preferred the less prosaic explanation. The anxiety I had palpably felt these last few days appeared to have morphed —doubtless under the influence of our plush surroundings and the romance that a train ride through the heart of Europe portended—into a relaxed acceptance of our circumstances and the expectation of a great adventure. I was probably being as overly optimistic now as I had been overly pessimistic before, but no matter. It felt good to be in control of my emotions, especially as the encounters of the next three days would require the utmost self-control and aplomb. We were chroniclers; we were John Reed. We would have to act with the wisdom of ancient Muscovite scribes and the derring-do of a rash American communist. Without, at the same, annoying each other or, worse still, having an affair.

The train started with a jolt. Pippa appeared to be dozing, so I left as I had come and ensconced myself before the writing table and opened my laptop. I scanned the news and learned that Russia was still in freefall and the non-Russians were still making advances. That crazy general who insisted he had nuclear weapons was threatening to use them, but what else would you expect from a crazy general? The Yankees had beaten the Red Sox and were now in first place. There was the usual mud-slinging, finger-pointing, and name-calling in Washington. Ho-hum, I thought, *plus ça change*. I heard a light knock on the door followed by a hushed announcement that lunch would be served in the dining car in half an hour. Cocktails were already available. I shut my laptop, washed my face and rinsed my mouth with mouthwash, and knocked on Pippa's door.

*

We were seated three tables from Pitun, who, surrounded by his beaming acolytes, appeared to be in excellent spirits. He directed a regal wave at us. We waved back. The train had picked up speed, but was much slower than the TGVs that approached two hundred miles per hour. Which was just as well. The unrolling landscape—jagged cliffs and ashen mountain tops adorned with pine trees, cactuses, and auburn-roofed villages—was delightful and I, for one, was resolved to enjoy every bit of the nostalgia on offer.

Immersed in the scene beyond the window, I didn't immediately notice Pippa's rising from her chair to greet the couple that joined us. It was only after I heard a booming "Howdy, y'all!" that I spun my head around to espy a husky man equipped with a stubby nose, sparkling eyes, a smile as broad as the state he was from (Texas, as I had surmised on the platform), and shoulder-length white hair. His wife, brandishing a full red mouth, hawk-like nose, and a bust as expansive as the state she was from, was equally imposing. Complementing their physical statures was an oversized friendliness that was no less commanding. I had encountered many such types in the States, but I could well imagine that the far more reserved Pippa would experience exquisite torture in their exaggerated company.

That said, there was nothing to be done but to make the best of the difficult circumstances. I took the initiative and introduced Pippa Tumblethwaite and me as journalists invited by none other than Vladimir Pitun to cover his return to Russia. The Texan's poor chair creaked under his size and weight as he settled into it. Distracted, I lost my train of thought and looked around uncomfortably.

"And you folks?" I enquired, resorting to what I assumed was their vernacular.

"I'm Lady Bird Houston and that there ginormous fella trying to fit his big rear into that tiny thing that passes for a chair is Bobby Lee Houston."

"We're in the oil business," he growled. Then, while suppressing a yawn: "Got here this morning."

"I take it," Pippa jumped in after a prolonged silence, "you're Pitun supporters?"

"Love that man," Lady Bird gushed. "I jes love him. We could use a president like that in our country. Ain't that right, Bobby Lee?'

"Damned right."

"The man's got a good sense of right and wrong, don't he, Bobby Lee?" Without waiting for an answer, she went on. "And he's always on the side of right—he shore is, that man. Why they tell me Russia was a"—she seemed to be searching for the right word—"well, it was like Mexico, wasn't it? And that lovely, gorgeous little man—he's so tiny, why I could just hug the breath outta him—he made Russia what it's supposed to be, right, Bobby Lee?"

"Damned right."

"And just what is it supposed to be?" Pippa asked, her eyes fixated on Lady Bird's heaving bosom. I nudged her gently with my elbow, fearing that she'd try to embarrass the Texans with her abrasive questions. Pippa, I knew, just barely tolerated what she termed "civilized" Americans (a category to which I, being a Yale-educated Connecticut WASP, just managed to belong), while her feelings about the "uncivilized" part—which encompassed most of the population outside certain neighborhoods in Boston, New York, Washington, and San Francisco—bordered on the genocidal. Alas, my nudge appeared only to increase her truculence and she repeated her question, but with stronger emphasis on the verb.

Lady Bird looked momentarily confused. She looked at Bobby Lee, but he was staring at the water glass and bread basket and proffered no help. "Well," she said hesitantly, "well—Oh, I don't know—well, it's obvious, ain't it?" Her face had lit up and

I could see that Pippa was going to get her comeuppance. "It's to be great, ain't it? Every great country should be great, right, dearie? Take the good ol' US of A. Take—"

"Texas," Bobby Lee volunteered.

"Jes what I was gonna say, Bobby Lee," she said triumphantly. "Y'all ever been out Texas way? The greatest state in the world. And y'all know why?"

Sullen, Pippa said nothing, while I refused to get embroiled in her fight.

"Cause we know it and act like it," Bobby Lee concluded, his reverie over and his devotion to monosyllabic utterances abandoned. He spoke with the finality of a judge delivering his verdict.

"There you go, Bobby Lee," she cried, taking his paw and squeezing it, "hitting that nail on the head once again."

Fortunately, a waiter came up to our table with a dumb waiter loaded with bottles and asked us what we would like to drink. Bobby Lee and Lady Bird both opted for Southern Comfort, double and neat, Pippa requested an extra dry martini, shaken but not stirred (a remark, obviously intended for my ears, that signified she had regained her sense of humor), while I resolved to keep my wits and ordered a beer.

"Not a drinking man?" Bobby Lee said. I thought I noticed a slight sneer in his voice.

I shook my head and lied, "Only in the evenings." I lifted my glass, said, "Cheers," and then, after they dropped their glasses onto the table, asked: "Pardon my journalistic curiosity, but I take it you're Pitun's backers?" I wanted to say *financial* backers, but decided against the modifier.

"No need to use them big words with us, son," Bobby Lee admonished me with a toothful smile. "This ain't our first rodeo. We may look like hicks, but we shore ain't hicks."

"We're American patriots," Lady Bird interjected, while Bobby Lee scowled. At her, I thought, thank God at her and not at me. In any case, he had, as his next comment revealed, understood what I was really asking.

"Like I was saying, we give our money to all kinds of good causes—charities, schools, poor folk, black folk, white folk, you name it, son, we support it. And sometimes, but only sometimes, we support politicians. Usually, I can't stand that breed. Cheats and liars and thieves, most of them. But then, once in a blue moon, an honest fella shows up, a man with gumption and integrity, a man I'd like to have my daughter marry. Know what I mean?" I nodded and, satisfied that I had understood, he went on. "And this here P'toon fella—well, this here P'toon fella is what we call a straight shooter. Know what that is, son? That's an honest fella. You can trust him with all your money, cause you know he'd never so much as take a penny." Because he's already embezzled seventy-five billion from the Russians, I thought. "And he's got ideas and I mean *big* ideas." Bobby Lee lifted his massive arms high above his head to illustrate the point. "He's the kind of fella that's gonna change the world—and I mean for the better. Ain't that right, Lady Bird?"

*

At that moment, we were saved, not by the proverbial bell, but by the high-pitched rapping of a knife against glass and our attention turned toward Pitun. The dining car had filled with our traveling companions and, surveying us all with a benevolent smile pinned to his mustache-less, goatee-less, and eyepatch-less face, he addressed us in Russian, with the trusty Voronov translating. He would be short, Pitun stated, as he knew how hungry we all were. ("You mean you *are* short," Pippa whispered into my ear.) This was the beginning of a revolution in Russia. The forces of evil and fascism—he mentioned the Chechens, Ukrainians, and Estonians by name—had dared attack Russia in a moment of weakness. They thought they would triumph, but they were wrong. The Russian nation was waiting for their savior to restore law and order and finally make the country as great as it deserved to be. And you, dear friends, he concluded, are all part of that great historical event. We, together with him, would make history. And all the peace-loving nations of the world, among whom the Russians would be first, would be grateful to us for all time.

"Let us make history!" he cried in conclusion. The crowd spontaneously responded, "Let us make history!" and then cheered and applauded for a good minute. Pitun looked embarrassed by so much acclaim and, his hands clasped as if in prayer, his head bowed, waited for the hoopla to end. Then, having said all he had to say, he cried, "*Priiatnego appetita!*" and returned to his seat.

It was, I thought, quite a performance. To be sure, he was preaching to the converted, but, even so, the enthusiasm was both unorchestrated and genuine. If his followers in Russia were only half as energetic, Pitun's restoration could be more than the clownish denouement of an inglorious career.

"What did he say at the end?" Lady Bird, her eyelashes aflutter, asked. "Sounded like ne-vo-tee-ta."

"*Priiatnego appetita,*" I explained. "That's Russian for bon appétit."

"You speak the lingo?" Bobby Lee looked impressed. "Me —can't make heads or tails of it. American is good enough for me."

I ignored that last comment and said, "German, too. And Pippa's French is excellent."

"Got no use for Krauts and Frogs in Texas. We saved their butts in the war and what thanks do we get for that? Zip."

I wasn't going to go down that road and, casting a stern glance at Pippa, stated, "Well, the president has spoken, so I suggest we dig in." King-sized, juicy steaks that probably testified to the esteem with which Pitun regarded the Houstons' deep pockets had appeared during his peroration and they looked delicious.

"Ne-vo-tee-ta appetite," Lady Bird dutifully repeated after bowing her head briefly and saying grace.

A few minutes and some vigorous mastication later, Bobby Lee pushed away his empty plate and looked me straight in the eye. "Steven Smith," he began, almost as if he were introducing himself and not addressing me.

"Yes?"

"Knew a fella by that name in the Agency. Way back when, during Nam. Your relation?"

"As a matter of fact, he was. My father's cousin."

"Good man," Bobby Lee affirmed. "Me and him served in the same unit."

"You mean in the army?"

"Nah, in the Company."

"In Vietnam?" I couldn't conceal my disbelief and surprise.

"Yep," he said drily. "Small world, ain't it? Whatever became of him?"

"Car accident about ten years ago."

"Sorry to hear that. Good man, yeah, he was a good man. And one helluva agent. Spoke Vietnamese, penetrated into Cong villages, saved my butt once. Yeah, I wouldn't be here if it wasn't for him. Good man," he concluded sadly, "one helluva good man." His mood suddenly changed. "You know, son, I tried to get him to join me in the oil business, but that sonofagun said he was married to the Company. He could've been a millionaire..." His voice trailed off and then, his eyes twinkling mischievously, it revived. "We had some good times together. That sonofagun could drink a platoon under the table! And when it came to the ladies—"

"Now, now, Bobby Lee," Lady Bird scolded, "you can keep those godawful stories to yourself. I'm shore Miss Pip-Puh don't care to hear how you sowed your wild oats!"

I glanced at Miss Pip-Puh, who responded with a demure smile and a no less demurely formulated question. "And you're still in touch with the Agency, Mister Houston?"

"With my pals, shore! Most have retired, but some are, I reckon, still active. Not in the field though. They've all been put out to pasture in Langley. The good Lord knows what they do there. I shore as hell don't."

Then came the inevitable follow-up: "And do they know you're here?" Pippa couldn't resist following a lead and this one, if corroborated, could be sensational. I could just imagine the lurid headline: CIA Supports Russian Dictator's Return.

Bobby Lee fell silent for a moment, perhaps realizing that he had, under the influence of the Southern Comfort and the perfectly grilled steak, disclosed a tad too much in his rambling reminiscences. Then, as if suddenly awakening from a deep sleep (it occurred to me that his momentary inattentiveness could have been induced by jet lag), he cried, "Oh, hell, no, Miss Pip-Puh! Why should they? We talk about fishing and baseball. Nah, Miss Pip-Puh, Mister P'toon is my *personal* investment. Ain't that right, Lady Bird?"

Before she could respond, Voronov rose from his chair and announced that one of our guests, the world-famous Russian soprano, Anna Trebenko, who also happened to be a fervent supporter of President Pitun's new Russia, would sing a few arias for our entertainment. I had heard Trebenko several times a decade or two ago, when she was in her prime. Now, she looked like an ex-diva: thickly applied make-up, extravagantly red lips, a sagging chin, and visibly dyed hair, which, when the light struck it at a certain angle, gave off a purplish glow. But, accompanied by the even rhythm of the train, she sang well enough (Mimi and Manon, her bravura roles in the old days) and made up for her inability to hit the high notes cleanly with verve and arm-waving. We burst into loud and prolonged applause after Trebenko finished, while she bent over the clearly pleased Pitun and, her ample breasts almost smothering him, embraced him tightly and planted several loud kisses on his bald head. He reemerged looking pale, but his triumphant smile quickly reasserted itself. As our attention reverted to our own tables, we noticed that the steaks had been cleared away and that chocolate Sachertorte and coffee and Cognac had been served.

"Oh," swooned Lady Bird, "I shore do love that Say-cher cake!"

I took my snifter and, wanting to end our conversation on a positive note, proposed a toast to the brave men and women who had defended America. "Hear, hear," said Bobby Lee. "The best of the best," added Lady Bird. Only Miss Pip-Puh failed to join our mutual admiration society and said, "To cloaks and daggers." I'm sure she meant it humorously, but our two interlocutors clearly failed to appreciate the joke. But, fortunately, it didn't matter, because, as they were parting, Bobby Lee whispered into my ear, "Stay in touch, son. You and that Miss Pip-Puh are good folk. We could use you."

Who the *we* were I hadn't a clue and didn't want to ask.

*

Back in my compartment—feeling somnolent, Pippa retired to hers—I noticed that we had long since crossed over into Italy and were barreling toward Milano, which we should reach in a few hours. After that, another four hours and we'd be in Zürich in the late evening, when a light supper was supposed to be served. That was to be followed by drinks and a *tête-à-tête* with Pitun. And, eventually, sleep. The Houstons had exhausted me and the steak had been the *coup de grâce*. I could hear Pippa's snore and, trying to harmonize that rhythm with the waltz-like beat of the train, I fell asleep. But I slept poorly. Images of the bloodshed in Moscow—and, bizarrely, of Lenin's glistening fingernail—continually asserted themselves; I heard screams, gunshots, and bomb blasts; I saw streaming crowds, angry mobs, and abandoned children with their hands miserably extended. And throughout, Andrus, who appeared to be my father, admonishing me for having abandoned my vocation and joined the enemy. A train whistle—we had entered a tunnel—brought me back to consciousness. Pippa was still snoring, so I crept into the bathroom, took a quick shower, and fortified myself with a large whiskey.

I watched the Italian countryside glide by, thinking of my first trip to Europe when, armed with a knapsack and a Eurail Pass, I had explored the entire continent in seven months. Those were the days before mass tourism made finding an empty seat in a train virtually impossible, when compartments seating eight were the norm, and when inexpensive pensions and one-star hotels were readily available for poverty-stricken students. I had managed to see Europe when it still consisted of a multiplicity of different nations with their own customs, currencies, and cuisines. Now, Europe had become a bland amalgam of similarly equipped places and similarly dressed people. Perhaps that was historical progress. Or perhaps that eradication of visible and invisible differences was a historical crime. In any case, I could take consolation from having seen the before as well as the after. That didn't ameliorate the sense of loss, however. That old world had been mine; this world belonged to everyone, which is to say to no one. The Russians believed their civilization was dying. Welcome to the club! I thought. We had begun decaying decades before you.

Pippa knocked on my door and I rose to open it. She was holding a drink in one hand and a bag of pistachios in the other. "I'll become an obese alcoholic if this keeps up," she groaned. "Will you still love me if I become a fat cow and reek of whiskey and sawdust?"

"More than ever," I replied. "Now sit down and let's talk."

"What dreadful people," she cried, "what absolutely dreadful people! If people like that can occupy a train like this, then it's—"

"—the end of the world? Agreed."

"The bloody end of the bloody world."

"Still, that bit at the end was interesting, wasn't it?" She nodded, her mouth bursting with pistachios. "It sounds fantastic, but it could be that the CIA is aware of this."

"They bloody well should be, the buggers!"

"Right," I concurred. "The question, I suppose, is whether Bobby Lee is simply serving as their eyes and ears or—"

"—are they in on the plot? Hmm, that would be too delicious, wouldn't it, ducky? Your intelligence service, the infamous CIA, in cahoots with Russia's mad tyrant." She was giggling uncontrollably. "Perhaps we should junk this whole thing and head for Hollywood?"

"Nice try, but it doesn't make any sense. Russia is our adversary. Every president knows that. And Pitun has been no friend of America for at least twenty years. Getting rid of him is something the Agency has probably been considering for decades. Why support his return *after* he's been gotten rid of by his own people and when his chances of success are slim? No," I shook my head, "it just doesn't make sense."

"A rogue CIA agent's plot?"

"Everything's possible, I suppose, but I'm still inclined to think they're just keeping tabs on Pitun. That makes sense. That's what I would do."

"Bobby Lee and the equally impossible Lady Bird as the eyes and ears of the notorious Central Intelligence Agency? I don't think so, love," she opined. "Not even you Yanks could be that daft."

"Well," I corrected her, "we could, but, in this case, I

think you're right. For all we know, one of the waiters is a CIA informer. As to the Agency's larger aims, I bet they're keeping their options, as they call them, open. If Pitun comes back to vast acclaim, if he mobilizes the counter-revolution, if, if, and if—the imponderables are many, but if all the ducks do in fact magically line up in a row—then Washington would want to be able to say that they hadn't been just bystanders, that they were in on the triumph, and so on."

Pippa summed up my muddled thinking perfectly: "Hoping for his demise while covering their butts in case it doesn't happen." And then, as an afterthought: "And the dreadful Houstons as the wrong people at the wrong place at the wrong time."

"Bingo." We emptied our glasses and I refilled them.

"Meanwhile, here's the latest from Russia. Almost forgot, hadn't you, love, that we're here on a mission?" She uncrossed her legs languorously (and suggestively?) and leaned forward, as if she had a great secret to impart. "Some twenty non-Russian territories in the Russian Federation have declared independence and proclaimed Russian to be a *lingua non grata* in their countries."

"The language of the great Lenin!" I exclaimed sardonically, recalling the great efforts the Soviets had made to impose what they claimed was the civilizationally superior Russian language on their unwilling subjects in the Soviet Union and Eastern Europe.

Ignoring my interjection, she continued. "And the local Russians—well, most of them—are fleeing to Mother Russia, while a few diehards have taken up arms." Her tone became serious. "I smell ethnic cleansing in the air. By both sides—and that could be a bloody mess."

"And what of the Estonians and the Ukrainians who attacked Russia?"

"Oh, they're merrily advancing, while the Russian armed

forces are simply melting away. It's quite extraordinary, if you think about it—almost a repeat of what happened when the Germans launched Operation Barbarossa in 1941. Push comes to shove and the glorious Russian army turns into a bunch of terrified deserters in short pants. Here, have some pistachios. I'm getting fat just looking at them. Anyway, the Ukrainian, Chechen, and Georgian armies appear to have joined forces in the Kuban and the Caucasus, while the Kazakhs and the Turkmen—can you believe it, Steven: even the Turkmen have gotten on the band wagon!—have sent their troops in supposed hot pursuit of Russian terrorists, as they call them, in the steppe lands to their north. Oh, and parts of Kaliningrad province have fallen to a joint Polish-Lithuanian offensive. How's that for an update?" she beamed.

"And what of the Russian contenders for power? Any news about that loony general with nuclear weapons?"

"The great General Fedotov hasn't made his move yet. He's still someplace in the Urals and still issuing daily proclamations of the apocalypse that will descend on Russia's many enemies if they don't desist from their scavenging forthwith." She extended her empty glass. "How about a refill, love? Cognac. And make it a double. Since I'm already a whale, I may as well be a tipsy whale."

"He's the only one who worries me," I said after pouring her and myself another drink. How many had we had? Three? Four? I had lost count. "Some of these Zhirinovsky types are crazy enough to prefer the end of the world to the end of their world. Now, I don't think Pitun belongs in that category—"

"Although he might."

"Indeed, he might. Still, I'm inclined to think he would prefer to have a realm in which he could continue to be the Sun King."

"But I could see his dropping a bomb or two on, say, Tallinn or Kyiv or Warsaw. Who's going to stop him? And what would the West do? Invade a chaotic country on its last legs? I don't think so. Which means that Pitun might have *carte blanche* to do whatever he decides needs to be done."

"He won't succeed," I contended with greater certainty than I possessed. The train had reduced its speed and I noticed that we were approaching the imposing Milano Centrale. "It's suppertime," I grumbled, "and I'm still not finished digesting that steak—or our two companions."

"I'm starved," Pippa countered. "That sneaky little waiter whisked away my steak before I could consume more than a bloody little morsel!"

"He probably noticed that you were on the excessively hefty side and should stick to pistachios."

"Swine."

"Pig."

"I'll be ready in five, love."

*

Fortunately, supper was a buffet and seats hadn't been pre-assigned, so, while Pippa stacked up on delicacies, I took a few slices of smoked salmon and some gorgonzola cheese and both of us seized a table that seated only two. The Houstons stopped by, with Bobby Lee slapping me on the back and Lady Bird planting a plump kiss on Pippa's pale cheek. "Ain't they the sweetest couple, Bobby Lee?" she gushed. "Y'all should tie the knot as soon as we get to that Peters-something town. Why, y'all are so sweet, I could jes eat y'all up!"

Pippa produced a pained smile, while I hoped to make a noncommittal gesture by raising both palms and shrugging. When they were out of earshot, Pippa proceeded to do a perfect imitation of Lady Bird's drawl and finished her performance with a most unladylike curse.

"They've gotten under your skin," I remarked. "Just ignore them, smile, and nod your head. Eventually, like all bad things, they'll go away."

"Huh!" she grunted. "You're not the one who was targeted with her bloody kiss." And Pippa reached for the napkin and rubbed her cheek vigorously. "Just as I thought," she said as she examined the cloth, "she left half her make-up and lipstick on me. If there's anything I hate—"

"I know," I said, "it's a slobbering Texan. Eat your caviar before it gets warm."

It was Rougement's turn to annoy us, as it dawned on me that this two-seater produced the antithesis of solitude by inviting well-wishings from everyone who passed us. He smiled his oily smile, greeted us with unabashed insincerity, mumbled something in French to Pippa, and bade us a good evening. "We should be in for a treat after the meal," he winked. "The President will speak." I winked back and wished him *bon appétit*.

Then came Voronov and, pausing for only a second, looked around nervously and enquired if everything was to our satisfaction. It was, we assured him, and he moved on, but not before winking.

Finally, the great man himself, Pitun, stopped by. His normally expressionless fish eyes were twinkling, possibly from the surfeit of alcohol that, as his breath suggested, he had ingested. With both hands planted on our table, his head swaying slightly, he leaned toward us and, finger raised, whispered, "I see you are making good friends with Khyustons. They—beautiful people, my kind of people. We will build great Russia together." At that, he nodded knowingly and, like Rougement, departed with a wink.

"What's with the bloody winking?" Pippa enquired after he left.

"Dunno," I ventured. "Must be infectious. Eat your fish."

We had to endure another five or so more greetings, but,

fortunately, none entailed an exchange of words and we were able to finish our meals in relative peace. Irritated and exasperated by the rest of the group, which was chattering and carousing as if they were on a Caribbean cruise for oversexed singles, I suggested to Pippa that we take a brief walk through the train station. She concurred and, after confirming with Voronov that we had an hour before Pitun's *tête-à-tête*, we hopped off the wagon and made for the cavernous interior of Stazione Milano Centrale.

"Who built this?" Pippa asked, her voice hushed, as if she were in a cathedral. "Mussolini?"

"The *duce* himself. Back in the early ninety-thirties. It was supposed to be a showcase for fascism."

"Well, it succeeded. Why, just look at this space!" she cried. "It's positively gigantic."

"Supposedly the largest in Europe. An espresso?" She nodded and we entered a café with a few young Americans occupying several tables. The fatigued waiter took our orders, brought the coffees in a few minutes, and insisted that we pay immediately.

"I traipsed through Italy before university," Pippa said wistfully. "Never made it to Milan, however. Always assumed it's just a big, smelly city. But this alone—the station, I mean—would have been worth a visit. I can see why so many Italians took a fancy to Mussolini's charms. This place"—she waved her right hand in a wide, gentle arc—"is breathtaking." When she finished, her hand landed on mine and squeezed it. "Thank you for bringing me here."

Despite the relatively late hour, hundreds of Italians and tourists crisscrossed the vast hall in which we sat. Some ran, hats in hand, coats flapping. Others walked with determined looks on their faces. A few couples strolled hand in hand. The younger set carried knapsacks, while their elders pulled suitcases. The hall resounded with their voices, shrieks, and yells, as well as their echoes, creating a cacophony that fully corresponded to the stereotype of Italy as an unremittingly loud country. And this was the civilized north. In the south, especially in such cities as Naples, Taranto, Palermo, and Bari, the chaos would have been even greater.

"Which parts of Italy did you traipse through?"

"Venice and Florence, of course—and Rome. Oh, and Naples, which was a madhouse, as I recall. A gorgeous trash bin, where the bloody waiters tried to charge us for the silverware and salt. And you?" she asked.

"Pretty much the same during that first trip. Afterwards, I've been up and down the country several times. Never fails to excite me. Even now—this station still sends a chill up my spine."

"Fascist swine," she snickered.

"Speaking whereof," I said, "we should be heading back to hear *il duce*'s words of wisdom."

*

I was expecting pablum and sloganeering, but, instead, Pitun treated us to a detailed analysis of conditions in Russia and the world. This was the Russian dictator at his best—a statesman who clearly knew his facts, had an operative strategic understanding of international relations, and a simple vision of Russia's place in the global order. Pitun was an unabashed authoritarian, possibly even a fascist, and an equally unabashed imperialist, who believed that Russian had a manifest destiny—he actually used the Russian equivalent of that term—and could only survive and thrive if it pursued it vigorously. As to the ongoing tribulations, they were, he assured us, temporary and would pass as soon as the Russian people and their non-Russian neighbors realized that law and order was being restored in his person and that all opposition to the popular will would be crushed.

"Mirabile dictu," Pippa whispered. "Did he just invoke Rousseau?"

"I believe he did." Unless, it occurred to me, he was rather more ominously invoking Russia's nineteenth-century terrorist organization, the *Narodnaya Volya* or People's Will.

Eventually, a reinvigorated great and powerful Russian state would retake its place in the sun. And the rest of the world will have no choice but to accept that reality, especially as, he suggested mysteriously, many leading countries had already told him privately that they hoped he would succeed and that they would provide him with targeted assistance, if and when the need arose. He didn't specify what kind of assistance that would be.

Things got a little fuzzier when he began expounding on his planned arrival in Russia. He expected Russians to turn out in the tens of thousands in St. Petersburg. Similar crowds were expected to assemble in all of the country's major and minor urban centers. His supporters were already organizing and mobilizing the population, apparently with great success. Once the rebellious non-Russians and the divided elites saw the extent of his support, they would fall in line and, with their support, he had no doubt that the glorious armed forces would expel the Estonian, Polish, Lithuanian, Ukrainian, and other invaders who had dared try to follow in the Mongols' footsteps and dismantle Russia.

"Mother Russia," he cried in conclusion, his voice hoarse and his forehead covered with sweat, "is invincible!"

The questions that followed his oration were mostly of the anodyne kind. People were either too tired, too stuffed, or too intimidated to ask for specifics—until Pippa's arm shot up and she stated, "But your army appears to have melted away, while the security service and National Guard are divided and fighting each other. Don't all your plans depend on having a well-functioning coercive apparatus, which is precisely what you don't have?"

Pitun, perhaps momentarily taken aback by the directness of her query, fell silent for a moment, brought his hands together and pressed them to his lips, and then spoke in oracular fashion. "I knew I did well in inviting you to be a chronicler." He surveyed his audience. "Ladies and gentlemen, that is Meess Peeppa Tambell-swayt and her colleague, Meester Steven Smees. They are both distinguished journalists who have graciously agreed to tell the world the truth about our campaign for Russia." The crowd applauded lightly. "As to your question, which is an excellent question, Meess Tambell-swayt, you are of course perfectly right. Our army is in some disarray and my first task will be to rebuild it. But that will be accomplished in two weeks, at most three. The soldiers, the national guardsmen, and the intelligence agents will rally to us as soon as they see that we are serious. And we *are* serious. They are all Russian patriots, somewhat demoralized at the moment—can we honestly blame them?—but ready and willing to save their country under my leadership."

The answer was a tad optimistic, depending on everything going just right, but it was an answer and not just propaganda. "Satisfied, Meess Tambell-swayt?" I whispered. "Quite," she answered. "Don't you have anything to ask him?"

"Naturally," I said and then, turning to Pitun, added: "And what of the international community and the West, Mister President? Will they support you?"

"No need to use the future tense, Meester Smees" was his enigmatic reply. "Please use the present tense—the very present tense."

Mine proved to be the last question and, after Voronov thanked Pitun and Pitun thanked us, the crowd dispersed. Pippa and I exchanged pecks on our cheeks, bid each other good night, and went into our separate compartments. I fell asleep immediately and dreamt only of endless numbers of Viennese couples doing the waltz to the rhythm of the train. I awoke when the waltz stopped and I saw that we were in Zürich, where Lenin's infamous journey in a sealed train had begun in 1917.

*

Our layover was to last a few hours, during which time supplies would be replenished, so, without waking Pippa, I stepped outside—it was unusually cold, but invigoratingly so—bought the *Neue Zürcher Zeitung* and *Financial Times*, and stopped for an espresso in one of the European coffee chains. Russia was still collapsing and the rest of the world was watching fearfully, but a small item on page ten of the *NZZ* caught my eye: there was a rumor that the president of Russia was planning to come back. Interesting, I thought. That was either the product of journalistic zeal or a cleverly planted signal to Pitun's supporters in Western Europe. Either way, its effect—heralding the coming battle—would be the same. Our junket was no longer a game or an adventure. Pitun and his people were playing for keeps.

"Now, why's a fine-looking man like you so serious?" It was Lady Bird and, having found her victim, she immediately resumed her twittering. "I've been walking back and forth and back and forth in this here big hall and all the time I'm thinking I know that fella and—ain't it something?—I do." She was bubbling over with excitement. "Ain't it been a swell trip so far? Why, I was telling Bobby Lee jes now, I said, Bobby Lee, this here has got to be the trip of a lifetime. Ain't that so, Mister Steven? I was reading in my guide book that this here town, Zirrick, was home to this crazy bunch of artists, oh, some hundred or more years ago, who called themselves Day-duh. You ever hear about them, Mister Steven? I was telling Bobby Lee about them and their antics and he laughed and laughed, saying they sounded like a bunch of Texas fellas he knew when he was in high school. You ever heard about them Day-duh fellas, Mister Steven?"

She wasn't expecting an answer, so, spared from having to deliver a lecture about the Dadaists, I glanced at my watch and said we needed to hurry back unless we expected to walk to Russia on foot. "Walk to Russia on foot?!" she cried. "Walk to Russia on foot?! Now, that would be something, wouldn't it, Mister Steven? You know what, Mister Steven? You're a hoot, Mister Steven, that's what you are, a real Texas hoot. I'll have to tell Bobby Lee, cause he's shore to appreciate it. Why you know, Mister Steven, this here train that we're on, why this here train moves so darned slow, don't it, Mister Steven? I wonder why. Do you wonder why? Is it cause of the Eye-talians running it? Back in Texas, we've got this mighty fine Eye-talian restaurant and, I tell you, Mister Steve, the service—why the service is just so darned slow you'd never imagine what they're up to in that kitchen of theirs. Why, you know what, Mister Steven?..."

I had stopped listening and, as she clasped my arm in hers and chattered on mindlessly, tried to coax her back to the train. She struggled to climb the steep stairs, even as I held her hand and pulled, but, her face red and flustered, she finally made it and, exhaling mightily, muttered something about the train being too small for Texans and, smiling sweetly and thanking me for being such a mighty fine gentleman, departed for her compartment.

I couldn't say I disliked the Houstons. There was something charming about their Texan manners and accent, about their naïve openness to the world, and their enthusiasm for so many things. But neither could I say I liked them. They were loud and overbearing and, frankly, embarrassing. Perhaps if they hadn't been American, I could've shrugged them off as anthropological curiosities, odd natives with odd customs. But they belonged to the same nation as I presumably did—which meant that we shared something in common. I couldn't imagine what it might be, but I knew the others probably viewed us as birds of a feather. And why should the opinions of this motley crew of suspicious characters and elegant dandies bother me? It shouldn't, and yet it did. Perhaps it was Pippa and her opinions that really concerned me. It was as if I had brought her home to meet the folks and crazy Uncle Ben happened to show up and tell his dreadful jokes.

It was amazing that, several days into our trip, Pippa and I hadn't quarreled even once. Indeed, we actually got along and I had to admit that I enjoyed her company. There were a few flirtatious moves, by her and by me, but nothing thus far that suggested that either of us wanted or expected or hoped for more. What better place to have a discreet affair than the Orient Express, amid its opulence, nostalgia, and romance? And yet, neither of us appeared willing to take a very short step and cross the invisible line between friendship and amour. Because we were journalists committed to our profession? Possibly, though that hadn't restrained me—and Pippa, certainly—in the past. Because the circumstances—our accompanying a bloody dictator to his dreams of revanche—weren't appropriate? But they never were. Or because we both sensed that this wouldn't just be a simple fling, but, instead, a serious—dared I use the word I detested and avoided all my life?—*relationship*? She seemed to have had a strained relationship with her parents; as a dyed-in-the-wool WASP, so did I. Was that the cause of our skittishness?

I slapped my cheek lightly. These thoughts were going nowhere or, in any case, they weren't going anywhere that I hadn't been to many times before. It was always the same—with the same result. I had affairs and flings galore, but avoided the R-word like the plague. And always would. So be it. I was a journalist, I was happy—well, more or less—with my life, and there was no reason to upset the proverbial applecart with some absurd *relationship*. Unless, of course, Pippa initiated it. Then we'd see. Or would we? Pitun, surely didn't have such self-doubts. He was a man of action who seized bulls by the horns and made decisions—sometimes rash, stupid, and counterproductive ones (his going back home being a case in point)—but at least he didn't spend his days scratching his bald pate and wondering what he should do. If nothing else, that characteristic went a long way to explaining his longevity. Someone incapable of crossing invisible and visible lines wouldn't have survived for more than a day in his position. But, notwithstanding my endless self-doubting, I did know one thing with complete certainty: I wanted another coffee and danish, so I requisitioned some in the dining car and returned to my compartment, where I went back to my reading and thinking. I found it oddly reassuring that Pippa's delicate snoring was just audible.

*

After she had finished her morning ablutions, Pippa knocked lightly on my door and stepped inside. She had requested that the waiter bring her breakfast to my room. Would I mind? Of course not, I said, pointing to the coffee cup and pastry crumbs. She was exhausted from the last two days' events and needed a temporary break from the other passengers. I nodded empathetically and told her that I felt the same way. A knock on the door followed and a waiter dropped off a silver tray.

"I bought real newspapers in Zürich," I said, handing them to her. "Smell them. Touch them. Heavenly, aren't they?"

"Positively divine," she swooned. I then told her of my unexpected adventures with the inescapable Lady Bird and Pippa gushed, her eyelashes moving like the wings of a hummingbird, "Why, Mistuh Smith! I do say Mizz Lady Bird has taken a mighty big fancy to y'all!"

"Heaven forbid," I moaned. I was going to say, "Mizz Tatyana, I do say you're jes a teensy bit jealous," but decided not to approach the invisible line, even in jocular fashion. "Well, anyway," I resumed my straight-man role, "I think we can expect more of her and the unsinkable Bobby Lee."

Pippa was devouring her third croissant and, with mouth full, mumbled, "But look on the bright side." Spirited chewing culminating in an audible gulp followed and then: "They'll make for great characters in whatever we write."

It was time to return to reality, so I changed the subject.

"What did you think of last night's performance?"

"Good start. The man is no fool. But then, when it came to details, especially after he arrives in Russia, rather thin. He either has concrete plans and doesn't want to make them public —"

"Which would make sense."

"—or he doesn't, which would be idiotic."

"And we're agreed that he's no idiot." I poured myself some coffee and took a sip. "Now, he's probably right that some, maybe even many, soldiers and agents and national guardsmen will rally around him. Why not? The other contenders are amateurs—"

"Except for that general with the bomb," she interjected.

"Exactly. Which leads me to believe that Pitun either has or is banking on that madman's support. Nothing would quite rally the troops around the flag like a nuclear weapon."

"And nothing would send as strong a message that Pitun means business as a nuclear detonation in—" she stopped and frowned. "In where? Kyiv? Pitun says the Ukrainians are really Russians. Tallinn? That might upset NATO. Almaty? Who knows what the Chinese will do?" Her eyes lit up. "Kazan!" she cried. "That's where I'd drop it. It's inside the Russian Federation, but a hotbed of Tatar nationalism."

"Or Grozny, the capital of Chechnya. They started the mayhem with the bomb blasts, after all. Besides, the Russians almost obliterated the place back in the nineties. Either one, actually. Take your pick."

"And the beauty of it all would be that the rest of the world would hold its nose and look the other way, the Russians could insist that they were forced to adopt extreme measures to deal with domestic terrorism, and the signal to all the non-Russians would be crystal clear."

"But would it work? Would Pitun win?" I shook my head slowly in response to my own questions. "I don't think so. Too much has happened and much of it is irreversible. Pitun and Fedotov could still kill millions and energize the demoralized *soldateska*, but the non-Russians are on the march—as are the Poles and Chinese. There are just too many countries aligned against a weak and demoralized, even if still savagely unpredictable, Russia."

Pippa was nodding her assent as I spoke. "You know, if we had some moral fiber, we'd do everything possible to stop him. I mean, if your analysis is right—and I think it is, ducky—then don't we have a moral obligation to do something?"

"Something? Maybe, but what?" I said weakly. "We're journalists, not freedom fighters. We fight battles with our pens and, as you know"—I couldn't think of anything better than a cliché—"the pen is mightier than the sword."

She screwed up her face and emitted a prolonged groan. "Is that the best you—*we*—can do? Resort to trite observations while the world is burning?"

I responded with another trite observation that only proved her point. "This isn't an Agatha Christie novel and neither of us is Hercule Poirot."

"Sadly, Steven, sadly," she said and reached for the last croissant.

*

Pippa read the newspapers, while I admired the Alps and the Bavarian landscape as we made our way to our next stop, Nürnberg, which we were supposed to reach in a few hours. Was Pitun aware of the symbolism? I couldn't be sure. He was generally quite knowledgeable about contemporary affairs, but his knowledge of history was probably deficient and colored by his intensely Russian perspective on all things. Did he know that the city was the site of Hitler's mass rallies? Or was he hoping to draw inspiration from imagining how the adoring German masses greeted their *Führer* and transferring that adoration onto the putative Russian masses eagerly waiting for him in Petersburg? More pointedly, did he recall that Nürnberg was the site of the Nazi war crimes trials—a fate that could, not implausibly, also await him, especially if his ambitious adventure imploded and he was subsequently dragged in chains to The Hague to face the music?

As much as I tried to focus on these questions, the beauty of Bavaria continually interfered and distracted me. I had vacationed here several times and had never tired of the mountains, forests, and lakes—as well as the culture and history nestled among the mountains, forests, and lakes. Unfortunately, the tourists had overrun Bavaria just as they had overrun Europe and much of the world. Now, cathedrals charged outrageous entrance fees, opera tickets had become exorbitantly expensive, and waiters actually expected tips. The world had changed—or was I simply getting old?

"Why the pensive look?" Pippa asked. "Recalling the days of yore? Or just suffering from a belated hangover?"

"A bit of all three," I answered. Then, more cheerfully: "You ever been to Bavaria?"

"*Jawohl, mein Herr*—but only in Munich and Nuremberg. For a series I did some time ago on the resurgent German right." She must have read my thoughts, for she immediately added: "I know they're strongest in the former East Germany. This was for historical background."

"The right-wing Germans love Pitun," I pointed out drily. "Not surprisingly, of course. He embodies everything they want to be and the system he's constructed in Russia is a kind of fascism with a—"

"—human face?" She snickered. "Well put, Steven. By the way, I ran into that creep Voronov and he told me"—the hiatus was obviously intended to enhance the dramatic effect—"and he told me we'd be taking on two German guests in Nuremberg. Any bets on who they might be?"

"He didn't say?"

"No, all very hush-hush, but, wink, wink, *sehr* important."

"Some socialist bigwig," I offered, "and a businessman. I'll bet you five euros."

"Some bet!" she snorted. "OK, I'll place my money on two wankers from the Alternative for Deutschland."

"Too obvious, my dear. I'm disappointed by your lack of originality. But very well: five-to-one odds on my bet and even odds on yours. Agreed?"

Ironically, as the train pulled into Nürnberg and three Germans boarded it just before we departed for Berlin, both of us proved to be right. I paid Pippa five euros and she handed over twenty-five.

"Not bad for a day's work," I quipped.

"Capitalist swine," she screwed up her face and pretended to snarl. "Just you wait, Henry Higgins, just you wait—when the revolution comes…"

CHAPTER FIVE

The Baltic Sea

The Germans joined us for lunch, a buffet affair with no assigned seats. They sat with Pitun and Voronov, while Pippa and I positioned ourselves at an adjacent table along with the two Russians from the Union of Patriots. The one we had met in Nice, the bald-headed Ivan Ivanovich Stepankoff, greeted us with a slight bow and a cordial smile that, as before, dazzled us with a set of sparkling white teeth. His colleague, a sallow-faced man with short brown hair, a reddish goatee, expansive nostrils, and deep-set tearful eyes, also bowed and introduced himself as Vladimir Lvovich Tolstoy.

"As in the great writer?" Pippa asked hopefully.

"*Hélas, non,*" he shrugged. "My namesake was a fine writer, *naturellement,* but, personally, I prefer Dostoevsky. He understood the Russian soul. He was strong."

"And Tolstoy was weak?"

He shrugged again, as if to say that so naïve a question couldn't possibly merit a response. Fortunately, Voronov spared us the continuation of what might have become an unpleasant exchange—I could see from the fire in her eyes that Pippa would have defended one of her favorite writers with tooth and nail—by introducing us to the Germans. A bald man with small eyes, wire-rimmed glasses, and a corduroy jacket with no tie said he was Erhard Kasselbach of the Socialist Party. The next one, expensively dressed and flashing perfectly contoured alabaster teeth and a massive gold watch, identified himself as Hanno Bierstadt of the German Commercial Council. The third, sporting bushy eyebrows, a luxuriant beard, and scruffy jeans, was Volker Schmidt of the Alternative for Germany. They bowed, we bowed; they smiled, we smiled; and then we all sat down. I couldn't speak for Pippa, but my heart was racing.

"Too many teeth," she winced. "My eyes hurt."

The most striking thing about the trio was that they were sitting next to one another on one side of a table. That implied equality and agreement and I was certain that they had consciously agreed to the symbolism. Even more astonishing, Voronov went on to say that the three were all fervent supporters of Pitun and his cause and that they had taken time from their exceptionally busy schedules to accompany us as far as Berlin and thereby demonstrate to the world—by which, I suppose, he meant Pippa and me and, possibly, the Houstons—that Germany stood behind Russia's legitimate president.

They were probably going to Berlin anyway, I thought cynically, but, even if so, this was an earthshattering development. The Socialists hated business and the right. Business hated the Socialists and was uneasy with the right. And the right-wing AfD hated everybody. And here, instead, representatives of all three camps were sitting together at a table, breaking bread, smiling courteously, and making nice with Pitun and, most importantly, us. Normally, they wouldn't be seen dead together in the presence of journalists, while now, *here*, they were actively and comfortably seeking the very coverage that was usually anathema to them. They fell silent after the introductions and resumed eating. At first, I was puzzled by their reticence, but then I realized that there was nothing more for them to say. Their very presence said it all. *O sancta simplicitas!*

"Are you thinking what I'm thinking?" Pippa mused.

Certain that she hadn't divined my lapse into Latin, I resolved to be cryptic in the presence of so many ears. "That the very fact of the three musketeers is a remarkable phenomenon?"

"Quite." She lowered her eyes and resumed picking at her shrimp salad.

The great democrat, Stepankoff, meanwhile, turned to me and unleashed his teeth. "I sensed skepticism ze last time vee spoke. Permit me to ask: Are you steel skeptical?"

I decided to play hard to get. "About what?"

"About prezeedent's chances for triumphantic return, of course."

"Was I really?" I persisted with the dance. "Honestly," I looked directly into his eyes, hoping that he'd blink—which he didn't. "I'm just following a good story. As to what my opinions are—heck, I'm not sure I even have any."

"Deeffeecult to believe. Everyone has opeenions. Een particular, journaleests."

"Well, since you insist, I believe I'll write a damned good story and possibly garner the Pulitzer." I was counting on his not knowing the verb and the direct object.

Stepankoff looked confused—evidently, my ruse had worked—mumbled something that sounded like "I am glad," grabbed his plate, excused himself, and headed for the buffet.

"One for the angels," Pippa whispered.

*

"Bloody Krauts!" Pippa exploded as I shut the door to her compartment. "Bloody, bloody, bloody Krauts! Did you just see that? The left, right, and center join forces and brazenly"— she spat the word out—"throw their support behind that little man, that, that—bloody *dwarf!*" She poured herself a Bourbon and downed it. "How dare they? How dare they betray their own country and everything the bloody Krauts have been doing since the bloody war for"—she actually sputtered a second time —"for, for that, that self-styled Napoleon?" She downed another drink. "That little bloody monster who's crushed all semblance of democracy and civil society in Russia, who's placed himself on a throne and crowned himself tsar—why, that bloody tyrant deserves to rot in jail—*no*, in *bloody* hell."

"Keep your voice down," I admonished. "They could be listening."

"No, I won't," she protested, but in a barely audible voice, and finally lowered herself onto her bed, her hands trembling and her face flushed. "And to think we're part of this obscene charade." She lowered her head penitently, as if awaiting absolution. "To think we're helping that bald dwarf attain his goals. You know what, Steven? I'm ashamed. I'm bloody ashamed."

"Don't be, Pippa," I said, hoping to soothe her with a display of insincere bravado. "We're just walk-on characters with no real role to play in this tragicomedy. It's Pitun's show—as well as Voronov's and those other creeps. We're just extras, two-bit players who strut and fret their hour upon the stage and then are heard no more." The Shakespeare had no visible effect, so I took her hands in mine and squeezed. "And besides, what we write will eventually determine how the world perceives Pitun and his actions. We can spoil everything if we write the truth. And we *will* write the truth, so what's there to worry about?"

We were pulling out of the station and, for a few seconds, I was mesmerized by the train tracks that seemed to be moving as quickly as we were, opening and closing and swerving, rhythmically and almost melodically opening and closing and swerving—like serpents under the spell of some genie. An appropriate image for the confusion Pippa and I were experiencing: we were racing ahead, driven by the wind, but without a clear sense of what still lay ahead and where we would end up.

Her nerves unrattled, Pippa reverted to her usually more reserved demeanor and removed her hands from mine. "Shouldn't we try to do something? And I know what you'll say: we're not Hercule Poirot or, for that matter, James Bond or—"

"Even sweet Miss Marple."

"Precisely," she said sharply, irritated by my interruption. "Shouldn't we try to, well—shouldn't we try to sabotage this whole"—she waved one hand as if trying to catch a fly —"thing? Isn't that our moral duty?"

"How? Tell me *how*." She said nothing, so I went on with my questions. "Perhaps we should push him off the train, huh? Or plant a bomb? Or take control of the locomotive?" I giggled as I shook my head. "We're powerless, Pippa—at least in this kind of way. We're not James Bond," I said flatly. "It's as simple as that. However—pour me another drink, will you?—however, we are not powerless in our own way. That bit about the pen being mightier than the sword is true—unless, of course, you're facing the swordsman at this very moment. We can make or break Pitun—not here, not on the train—but later, when we get off and he'll need all the press he can get."

"By then he won't care," she replied glumly. "If his plan works, even so far as to be greeted by adoring crowds in Petersburg, he'll be able to do whatever he likes. And if that lunatic General Fedotov throws in his support and if the soldiers take up their guns and join up—then, Steven, all bets are off." She opened another bottle and filled my glass. "I know, I know, he won't win and you're probably right. But just think at what cost. About three million people died during the Russian Civil War in 1918-1921. It could be just as many, probably more, this time around." She looked at me pleadingly. "I'm right, you know."

I nodded. Russia was already self-destructing and Pitun would likely accelerate the process and raise the number of casualties severalfold. The Soviets used to talk about the iron laws of history as making the victory of communism inevitable and transforming the efforts of individual human beings into the beating of a butterfly's wings during a tornado. Pitun thought he controlled history. He believed that he, like Napoleon and Lenin and Stalin, had a world-historical mission. He was certain he would triumph. In reality, he was but history's pawn and, at the end, when the dust will have settled and the rubble will have stopped bouncing, he would, if still alive, see that his efforts did nothing less than bring about Russia's—and his own —final and irreversible destruction.

"It's a job for the Russians," I said. "They have to decide whether they want to go down in flames with him or with some sense of honor without him. We—you and I and everybody on the outside—can only watch and sigh and shed a tear or smile."

"I'll shed a tear."

"I'll shed a tear and smile," I said. "Russia has outlived itself. It was the world's last empire and, sooner or later, its extinction was—*is*—inevitable." And then, for added effect: "And that's probably a good thing."

"And what of Russian culture? Of Tolstoy and Dostoevsky and Pushkin and Tchaikovsky? Not to mention Solzhenitsyn, Mayakovsky, and Akhmatova?"

"Oh," I said matter-of-factly, "they'll survive. Good culture always does, doesn't it?" The question was rhetorical, so I didn't wait for her response. "I can easily imagine that, once Russia the imperial state joins the ash heap of history"—"the phrase is Soviet," I said in response to her quizzical look—"once it alights the ash heap of history, the language, the arts, the music produced by Russians will probably enjoy renewed popularity throughout the world." Her face brightened. "Think of the irony, Pippa. Pitun tried to spread the language and culture by force—and failed. After all, who wants to speak the language of an aggressor? And because force will prove to be his and his country's undoing, the language and culture will survive and probably thrive!"

"On bookshelves and in museums, ducky, only on bookshelves and in museums."

"And—pardon the mawkishness—in the hearts of Russians. Don't forget the Russians, especially the decent ones. They, too, will survive."

Did I believe what I had just uttered? Probably, though I wasn't certain I cared as much as I implied. Moreover, I knew I felt a bit of *Schadenfreude* at Russia's travails. If any country deserved to collapse for having imposed its barbarian values on half the world, it was Russia. And if any people deserved punishment for their arrogant behavior and idolatrous adulation of a dictator, it was the Russians. But the *Schadenfreude* was of modest proportions, as I also realized that my critical sentiments toward Russia could as easily apply, were I to be objective, to my own country. As well as, for that matter, to Pippa's.

To be sure, the collapse would entail enormous losses of human lives and that was tragic. But the Russians themselves had brought that tragedy upon themselves, just as the Germans had done in the nineteen-forties. And perhaps, like the Germans, the Russians would draw the appropriate lesson and realize that peace is preferable to grandeur. Naturally, that transformation could happen only if Pitun lost—which made it all the more imperative that we ensure that the world learn the truth about him. I expressed that last sentiment to Pippa and, in a gesture that connoted both agreement and uncertainty, she shrugged, nodded, and raised her eyebrows.

Then she said, "If we know that, then so, too, must Pitun. He can't be so naïve as to believe that we're on his side." She furrowed her brow. "Now, if *I* were *he*, I'd stage as many photo-ops with us as possible, make sure they do the rounds of the world press, milk us for all the propaganda he can—and then dispose of us."

Unnerved by what I thought she was implying, I enquired, "What do you mean by dispose of us?"

"Arrange a tragic accident. Or, failing that, have one of his thugs—," and she pulled her hand across her throat.

"You can't be serious." I spoke unconvincingly and I knew it. And then even less convincingly: "He wouldn't dare. Why, you and I are—"

A loud knock prevented me from finishing my anodyne hope. A second later, a female voice announced, "Hello, dearie, it's Lady Bird and Bobby Lee. May we come in?" Without waiting for an answer, they burst in like a hurricane and, although part of me was resentful at the intrusion, most of me was glad to have had our doleful conversation brought to a sudden, if inconclusive, end.

"Did we intrude on a funeral?" Bobby Lee cried.

"Y'all look like you've seen a ghost," Lady Bird said. "Well, we shore are glad that we came when we did, ain't we, Bobby Lee? Our favorite couple needs some cheering up and we're the folks to do it to you!"

"And to tell y'all the truth," Bobby Lee continued, "these folks here are jes too European for folks like us. Too stuffy, too formal-like—and me, I like Americans best of all, don't I, Lady Bird? We're down to earth, ain't we, honey, even when some of us, like this gal Pip-Puh here, ain't quite hundred-percent American."

The pained expression on Pippa's face had progressively vanished and she even managed a snicker when Bobby Lee finished speaking. As much as I knew that she couldn't stand the Houstons, I also knew that she, like me, was positively delighted by their appearance. Their overbearing, gargantuan characters sucked up all the air in the compartment, their accent and abbreviations grated on my nerves, but these very same qualities also created an impression of absolute security. No one, not even a troop of Pitun's thugs, would dare do anything to us in their larger-than-life presence.

Pippa poured us drinks and then Lady Bird and Bobby Lee took turns relating bawdy jokes, howling before they reached the punch line, slapping their knees, and consuming the liquor with awe-inspiring alacrity. I stopped listening and simply followed the cues and laughed when called upon, but, this time, I found their incessant chattering to be comforting. It blocked out the world, diverted my attention from unpleasant scenarios to nothing in particular, and suggested that nothing could ever penetrate the noise they were generating. I still couldn't comprehend how such simple—or did I mean simple-minded? —people could possibly support Pitun. Nor could I understand how they could think so highly of him. Nor, finally, how their paths could have possibly crossed his. They were sympathetic loudmouths and harmless knuckleheads as well as foolish fellow travelers. And for present purposes, the first two features outweighed the third.

*

"I dare say," Lady Bird narrowed her eyes and peered out the window, "I dare say we're in Berlin, ain't we, Mister Steven? Why, we shore are! There's a sign, as big as Texas, and it says in big white letters—B-E-R-L-I-N. Y'all been here before, Miss Pip-Puh? Mister Steven? First time for me and Bobby Lee, though I dare say we ain't gonna see much, are we? I do believe we're jes dropping off the Germans and stocking up on supplies. Ain't that right, Mister Steven?"

The train ground to a halt and the stewards shuffled along the corridors announcing that we'd be making a one-hour stop. I was going to suggest that all four of us disembark and stretch our legs, but Bobby Lee leaned toward me, grabbed my knees with his hands, and said, "How about us two boys take a walk and leave the gals alone? You won't mind, will you, honey?" Lady Bird shook her head vigorously and, as much as I hated abandoning Pippa, the prospect of her having to cope with this garrulous force of nature amused me and I couldn't resist a wink as we exited the compartment.

"Don't mind Lady Bird," he began once we were on the platform, "she's one mighty fine woman, but, jes between us boys, she can sometimes be too much. I thank you kindly for tolerating her, son."

"Well, no, no," I stuttered, taken aback by his frankness,

"why, no, I'm sure I speak for both of us when I say we find your wife to be delightful."

"You're a bad liar, son," he chuckled, his eyes twinkling, "but I thank you kindly for your tact. Heck, even *I* find Lady Bird to be too much! But she's one good woman and one wonderful wife. To tell you the truth, I don't know as I'd be where I am without her. She's been on my side every minute of every day ever since we got hitched. Close to forty years now. Not bad for an old fart like me, eh?"

He placed his heavy arm around my shoulders and pulled me toward him. "You're one mighty fine sonofagun, Steve." Then his voice turned serious. "Don't think I haven't noticed that neither of you has pressed us on the P'toon business." I was about to protest, but he went on. "It's all about oil, son. Personally, I don't give a hoot about P'toon or any of his plans for Russia. To tell you the truth, I ain't even shore I like the fella. Those beady eyes... Not shore I could trust anybody with beady eyes. But we signed a whole bunch of deals with him and, if he's out, that means I've gotta renegotiate all those contracts with Lord knows who. Will the new fellas be more honest? Will they want bigger bribes? Who the hell knows? See what I mean, son? I've got a stake in P'toon and I've got to do everything I can to keep that investment safe." He released me from his hold and I inhaled deeply. "See what I mean, son? I'm caught between a rock and a hard place. If I do nothing and P'toon wins, I look bad. If I play along, like Lady Bird and I are doing, and he loses, the next fella who runs Russia will have my hide."

I nodded sympathetically. "Yes, I understand." And, as a matter of fact, I did. One could question Bobby Lee's moral judgment for having gone into business with Pitun in the first place, but he was a businessman and, as I well knew, that breed of human being always placed ethical questions on the back burner. Some of them were greedy, of course, but most of the ones I had met were decent types who needed to subordinate politics and morality to the imperatives of the market and its cutthroat rules. The arm suddenly reappeared, cutting my ruminations short.

Bobby Lee pressed me to himself again. "I'd like to ask you something, son. I like you. I'm a straight shooter and I say what I think. I think you'd be just the fella I need in my business. Any interest, son? See, I need a good negotiator, a good diplomat, but not some wishy-washy Washington man who can't look you in the face and who's got no grit, no backbone. But you, son, you got those qualities. Heck, if you'd be interested, you could even bring Miss Pip-Puh along. She's good people, too." He snickered obscenely. "Don't think I haven't noticed. And don't think I haven't noticed how y'all look at each other like a pair of lovebirds!" He slapped himself in the forehead. "Hey, I jes had a great idea! Why don't you two tie the knot? We could do the ceremony down in Texas—and I can guarantee you, boy, that it'd be like nothing you ain't never seen before!"

Shocked and struck quite dumb, I produced a crooked smile and took a deep breath, but said nothing.

"Ah, I've embarrassed you, ain't I, son? Why, heck, you're all red! That means I'm speaking the truth—about Miss Pip-Puh, I mean. As to the other business, think about it. Sleep on it. Heck, it ain't every day that someone offers you the opportunity of being my main oil man in Russia!"

"Russia?" I actually gulped audibly. The prospect of living in this godforsaken land was nowhere near the top of my priorities in life.

"Why, shore!" he cried. "Don't need you in Texas, son. But here, right here is where I could use someone like you. You know the country, you speak the lingo, heck, I bet you know the way these folks think, right? And then that P'toon fella likes you, which would make your job and mine a whole lot easier."

"If he wins."

"Well, shore—if he wins." He cast a quick glance at his

watch. "Whoa! We gotta be heading back. Train leaves in ten minutes and Lady Bird will be expecting some German chocolate. Maybe you want to get your lady friend something, too?"

Bobby Lee picked up a giant Milka chocolate with nuts and raisins; I opted for several newspapers and magazines. "You brainy types," Bobby Lee snorted. I blushed again and we made our way back to the train. The irrepressible Lady Bird was pacing nervously on the platform. "Why, I dare say I thought you boys had found yourselves some German froy-line!" she quipped. "Now, look here, Bobby Lee, it's high time you stopped chewing Mister Steven's ear off. He shore looks like he could use a rest and—oh, what's that? Now, you sweet old thing, you, why, you bought me a chocolate!" And with that she took his hand and led him into the train car. Pippa's face was pressed against the window and, as I waved in greeting and pointed to the newspapers, she made a face and stuck out her tongue.

*

"Can you imagine?" I started. "He wants me to work for him! Me an oil man! I hadn't the heart to put him out of his misery..."

"Would be lucrative," she smirked, "and you'd always be able to fly first class. In addition to buying yourself some nice ties. Finally."

Unable to think of a clever repartee, I changed the subject and asked, "And what did you two corn-bred gals talk about?"

Pippa emitted a prolonged groan interlaced with a few chuckles. "The poor dear. She occupies a world somewhere out there in deepest space. I actually came to feel sorry for her, but not in a pitiful, pathetic kind of way, but in a loveable kind of way. The old girl's absolutely batty!" I slowly elevated my eyebrows in mock surprise. "You know what she spent forty-five minutes trying to convince me to do?" I shrugged. "To marry *you*, you idiot!" That pointed remark was accompanied by a loud—too loud, if you ask me—snort. "What a nice couple we made. How she could see you were mad about me and I was mad about you. How we'd have the loveliest kiddies. Forty-five minutes of that, Steven, forty-bloody-five. While you were parading along the train station and chatting up the froy-line, I had to endure a lecture from my mother! Still," she continued after taking a deep breath, "she's a sweet old thing at the end of the day. Means well. Tries hard. Wants the world to be as happy as she is. But crazy as a bat. No, not crazy, just a bit loony. I had an aunt like that. We all loved her, even though—or was it because?—she lived in a world of her own."

"So, did you cave? Are we getting hitched?" It was my turn to smirk and hers to be tongue-tied.

"Oh, just hand me a newspaper and shut up, you bloody Yank!"

Yet again, the news hadn't changed much since we last consulted the papers. The bombings, shootings, fighting were still going on. Riots, by Russians, no less, had spread to a variety of provincial cities, though it was unclear just what or whom they were rioting for or against. It didn't matter, as chaos bred chaos and violence eventually bred violence of all against all. The most important item concerned General Fedotov, who announced that he was organizing an army in St. Petersburg, where he also awaited the imminent arrival of "Russia's rightful ruler." Was he being coy about Pitun? Was he suggesting that the rightful rule was someone other than Pitun? Was the vagueness a bargaining chip for use in subsequent negotiations with Pitun? Or did he and Pitun agree to leak only part of the story so as to raise expectations among the faithful, but not too much?

"You're becoming Russian," Pippa observed sourly, "reading tea leaves and looking for clues in every single word some idiot utters. It's probably just the way the story was written."

"But Fedotov *is* heading for Petersburg," I cautioned. "That part seems true."

"Which is what we expected, didn't we? Loon meets loon. It was a match made in heaven." She flung the papers onto the bed and stared into my eyes. Bobby Lee had exhausted me and I was desperate to avoid any serious discussion of politics. Instead, Pippa assumed a thoughtful pose. "May I ask you something?" I nodded, completely oblivious of the bombshell that she was about to throw.

"Will you spend the night here tonight?"

Without even hesitating for a second, I replied, "You know it's a dreadful idea."

"I know," she answered with no less firmness. "It's the worst possible idea at the worst possible time." An extended interlude followed and then came the inevitable follow-up: "So, will you?"

What could I say? I had hoped to hear that question on a train for much of my adult life. An enigmatic girl, preferably dressed in black, an immediate attraction, the speed of the train, the rhythmic churning of the wheels—and a furtive assignation in the coal-dark night. I had conjured up that scene many times, especially in my youth, and it remained lodged in my imagination all that time. And now, finally and half-unexpectedly, Pippa had popped the question. What could I possibly say in response?

Desperate for some dilatory tactic, I knew I was spared an immediate response when I heard her stomach growl. That unearthly sound was my cue and, taking her hand, I said, "Let's talk about it over some food," and, despite her feigned protestations, dragged her to the dining car.

The supper was delicious, but uneventful, as I easily managed to divert our conversation to the other diners and their attire. Bobby Lee stopped by for a minute and gave us what turned out to be an exceptionally fine bottle of California wine. Uncertain of what to do or say, we focused on the wine and, after consuming most of it, returned to our suite sooner than expected. I told Pippa I'd come over after taking a shower and we both retired to our separate compartments.

A minute later, a frantic knocking shook the door. Pippa burst in, visibly distraught, and cried, "My laptop's gone!"

"Are you sure?"

"Of course, I'm sure. It was on my bed. You saw it yourself." She looked around excitedly. "And yours? Where's yours?"

"Why, it's in this drawer." I pulled it open: there was nothing inside. "Our dear friend Pitun has evidently decided to get serious with us." I was going to suggest that we accost Voronov immediately, but Pippa, seemingly reading my mind, suddenly became the embodiment of serenity and, suppressing a yawn, advised, "No use complaining, Steven, they'll deny everything. Besides, we can speak to him tomorrow."

"I'm surprised you're so self-composed."

"So bloody tired," she murmured sleepily. "The bloody computers can wait."

"But they obviously suspect something," I said. "Did you have any compromising materials on your laptop?"

"No, just a few old stories, some notes, some photographs... nothing important."

"Me, too. Still, this is worrisome, Pippa." I felt a languorous fatigue take hold of me.

"Tell me something I don't know." She covered a cavernous yawn with her hand and smiled weakly. "Lord, am I ever tired!"

I took her in my arms and, barely suppressing a yawn, mumbled, "Perhaps—well, maybe you'd like to stay here?" She shut her eyes dreamily and yawned again. *Otia dant vitia*, I thought, leisure begets vices...

*

Next morning, a light knocking on the door awoke me. It was Voronov and, apologizing endlessly, he explained that one of the stewards had been caught stealing and that two weather-beaten laptops were found in his trunk and the first thing that occurred to him, Voronov, was that the machines probably belonged to people who used them in all sorts of circumstances —namely, Pippa and me. If we'd be so kind as to join him in his compartment after breakfast, he'd gladly give them to us. Naturally, the steward would be handed over to the authorities as soon as we reached Petersburg. Expressing a thousand apologies, he bowed and excused himself, leaving me puzzled about what had just transpired. Was the Frenchman really a thief? Or was this Voronov's not inelegant way of returning goods stolen by his own people?

As I contemplated both questions, while being unable to provide a convincing, definitive answer to either as a result of the exceptional heaviness in my head, I suddenly realized that the rhythmic waltz of the train wheels had ceased. Instead, we were rocking gently from side to side. I stepped into the corridor and peered out the window. Ash-gray water and swirling diaphanous mists surrounded us, while small waves lapped against the side of the barge that carried our train. The dough-like sky seemed to press on the sea, obliterating the horizon and transforming the faraway twinkling of lights into distant galaxies. We appeared to be on board a ghost ship heading for oblivion.

We must have reached Lübeck sometime at night and transferred onto the barge noiselessly. The excessive and virtually non-stop drinking, the emotional exhaustion produced by another extended session with the Houstons, the flirtation with Pippa, the fatigue induced by our extended confinement on the train, and the depression that followed our realization that our laptops had been stolen had all come together, almost as in a perfect storm, to make me impervious to the little noises that would normally have jolted me out of Somnus' sleepy realm.

My thoughts crept back to the computers. Why would a steward have purloined two old laptops? It made no sense, especially as he would have been far better off snatching the many Rolexes on parade or the jewelry worn by Lady Bird and the other ladies. No, it had to be Voronov and Pitun's other thugs. Even if they found nothing of interest in the computers, the mere fact of the theft had served to intimidate us—well, certainly me—and warned us about the possible future consequences of ill-considered behavior on our part. They might also have planted tracking or listening devices inside the machines.

A sleepy Pippa tapped me on the shoulder. "Couldn't you sleep? I slept like a bloody log." She rubbed her neck and temples. "And my head's all woozy, almost as if I'd been drugged."

"That's odd," I noted, "I slept like a log as well and my head's as heavy as an anchor. You don't think we were drugged, do you? Perhaps during supper?"

"But why would they drug us *after* taking our laptops?" She shook her head slowly and deliberately. "The logical sequence should have been first the drugs, then the theft. These chaps can't be that incompetent!"

I then related Voronov's story and my skepticism about the steward's guilt. "But I disagree," she opined, her sleepiness having suddenly vanished. "French stewards, like their Italian brethren, are notorious for being venal and corrupt. Remember the bad old days when you couldn't travel to places like Nice or Rome without having your bag grabbed by some hooligans on a moped? And the thefts that took place on the trains! I could regale you with stories that would disabuse you of your skepticism." A mighty yawn followed. "So, yes, I do believe that Voronov's tale is perfectly plausible, ducky."

I wasn't quite persuaded, so I retorted, "And our yawning last night? Our fatigue? Our heavy heads? And it was you who said you felt like you'd been drugged."

"Just a figure of speech, love. As to the rest, just look at those clouds. The barometer must have gone through the floor. Blame the low air pressure, not Pitun—well, at least not this time."

She was probably right—she usually was, after all—but I remained suspicious. There was too much espionage in my family's blood.

"Where's Germany?" She rubbed her eyes and yawned yet again. And then a sudden epiphany followed after she realized we were floating on water and cried, "When did we get on this bloody barge? It *is* a barge, isn't it? Good Lord, I slept like a log."

"You already said that," I pointed out.

"So, is this the North Sea?"

"That's on the other side of Denmark. This is the Baltic Sea. Germany or possibly Poland is to our right, Sweden is to our left. Eventually, we'll pass Kaliningrad, Lithuania, Latvia, and Estonia, wiggle into the Gulf of Finland, finally dock at St. Petersburg. It's about seven hundred miles as the crow flies. Probably about eight hundred in real miles. If you figure we're doing about five-six miles per hour for twenty-four hours, then —good God, Pippa!—we're likely to be on this tug for some six days!"

"Six days with the bird lady?" she cried, as her eyes grew large and again lost all trace of sleepiness. "I'll go bonkers. Her squawking will drive me positively, absolutely, completely bonkers." Then, her eyes narrowed and she declared, "I just had a thought. Do you think Pitun knows? I mean, is it possible he just made his first really big mistake? Fedotov is probably expecting him to arrive any day now and, instead, our boy is trapped on a barge in the middle of the Atlantic!"

"The Baltic," I corrected her. "Unless—unless we're headed for Kaliningrad, which must have some special arrangements regarding train traffic with the Baltic states. It's the Poles that wouldn't want to let us through for any price. But the Balts could probably be pressured—or bought. And then we'd be in Petersburg in about two-three days."

"And I won't be tempted to kill Lady Bird." Pippa yawned deliciously again. "Let's have some breakfast. I need a coffee. And let's get our computers back. I feel naked without mine."

*

When Voronov later explained just which route we would take, my hunch proved correct. The Poles had refused passage—back in 1917, the train passed through German-occupied territory as it carried Lenin and his comrades toward their encounter with revolution—and the barge, though slow, would get us to the former Königsberg—the city of Immanuel Kant and Johann Gottfried von Herder, he beamed proudly—whence, after a short stop to regain our land legs, we'd continue to St. Petersburg. And destiny, I wanted to say, but didn't. After again apologizing profusely for the unfortunate accident with our computers, he asked whether we'd like to have a private audience with the president, who could spare thirty minutes after breakfast. Naturally, Pitun wished he could spend more time with the world press, but important affairs of state never failed to get in the way. We understood, of course, didn't we? Of course, we did, of course, we did, we assured him. The audience was doubtless Voronov's way of unruffling our feathers for the temporarily missing computers.

We ate quickly, and anxiously, waiting for the signal from Voronov. Just as we finished our coffee, he waved at us from the other end of the dining car and we followed him to Pitun's suite. Ours had been luxurious, but this one took the cake. The bed cover was a rich red silk; the floor was made of red marble; the handles and door knobs all appeared to be made of genuine gold; and completing the outrageously over-the-top ensemble was a red velour wallpaper featuring gold-embossed designs resembling two-headed eagles. They must have outfitted the compartment specially for Pitun—and in the few night hours before his decision to take the train and our departure. That, I thought, bespoke no small clout. Whatever the case, his taste clearly bordered on the extreme, reminding me of the overblown palaces favored by celebrities in Beverly Hills, while at the same time heralding his reassertion of tsardom—as well as stardom.

He shook our hands, told us to pour ourselves drinks—which, against our better judgment, we did—and then hopped onto the bed, muscular legs outstretched, where he sat, smiling his Cheshire cat smile and cradling a glass in his hands. "*Strelaite*," he commanded, "shoot."

Pippa began with a question about the three Germans, saying that the symbolism of right, left, and center joining forces hadn't escaped her. Pitun slapped his thigh and said he knew he had done well to invite us along. Then, he went off on a ten-minute declamation on the historical longevity and strategic importance of German-Russian ties. Did we know that German had been used extensively at Peter the Great's court and that many Russian intellectuals studied at the university in Königsberg? The Germans had been one of the first nations to appreciate the genius of Russian literature in the nineteenth century, while the Russians had always looked with awe at the nation of poets and thinkers. And the Baltic Germans—why, they had served in many elite positions in the Russian army and state. Yes, to be sure, the twentieth century had been less amicable, but, since 1991 and the tragic collapse of the world's first experiment in socialism, Germany and Russia had enjoyed almost uninterrupted camaraderie and true friendship. So, who else but the Germans should support his return? It made sense, politically, culturally, and historically. In fact, he smiled, it was almost an inevitability—just as his resumption of power was also an inevitability.

Pippa sat impatiently as he conducted his monologue, so, as soon as he seemed to be finished, I leapt in with a question about General Fedotov: Was he the president's main ally? He seemed to be, but could Pitun please clarify? Five minutes were devoted to the harmonious relations between the political leadership and the military during Russia's existence since Ivan the Terrible. Then, as if sensing that both of us were restless with his historical excursions, Pitun switched gears and, choosing his words carefully, spoke about Fedotov. He was, he assured us, a good man and a good general, one of his best. He could count on his loyalty and trusted him with his own life. Moreover, Fedotov was beloved of his men. He never adopted airs and always shared the rank and file's miseries. The men loved him and trusted him and they knew that, when he called them to arms, they had no choice but to follow. Thus, concluded Pitun, his promise that he would collect a large army that would reestablish law and order and regain the lost territories was no bluff. He, Pitun, fully expected thousands of soldiers to have already assembled in Petersburg. They were armed and they were eager and all they wanted was a signal to begin the counterattack. And that signal was, of course, Pitun's arrival in Petersburg and the wildly enthusiastic greeting he would receive from the exultant Russian masses.

"Expect flowers and wreaths," he said with unconcealed pride. "We Russians know no bounds to our love—especially when the love is deserved."

Three knocks on the door led Pitun to consult his watch and pronounce, "Alas, dear friends, our time is ended. But I hope we will have an opportunity to chat one more time." And with that, he nimbly jumped off his bed, pumped our hands, and opened the door. We exited like two school children who had just had a session with the principal. Voronov was waiting outside with our laptops in his hands. He apologized yet again and handed them over, saying he fully expected that such embarrassing and unacceptable incidents would happen no more.

"That almost sounded like a veiled threat," Pippa whispered as we entered the dining car. "Or am I getting paranoid?"

"A second breakfast?" I countered. "I could stand a coffee and something sweet."

"*Moi?*" she said, lowering her gaze with exaggerated modesty and fluttering her eyelashes, and we claimed our former table and, having nothing better to do, gorged ourselves on the delicacies on offer.

*

The formerly dull sea had acquired some sprightly blue and green hues and the waves resembled the white-crested ripples in Impressionist paintings. The gulls, now as before, lazily circled the barge, gliding on the wind currents, emitting lonely moans that perfectly matched the desolate surroundings. The coast to our right was barely visible, almost fully enveloped in a silky mist that occasionally revealed clumps of olive-green trees and gleaming roofs. Disrupting the sense of utter isolation in some watery limbo were the silent ships and rusty tankers that plowed through the waters to our left and right. Despair flourished in such an atmosphere of emptiness and hopeful thoughts and expectations atrophied like leaves on dead branches.

I realized I was getting impatient with the trip and actually yearned for a return to whichever normality existed outside the confines of the train. Another two or so days and we'd be in St. Petersburg and all that we had experienced since boarding the train in Nice would recede into a soon-to-be-forgotten past that we would fondly recall by asking, "Do you remember?" It was close to two weeks now since I had arrived in Estonia. And what a time it had been! I had witnessed the horrors besetting Moscow, traveled to Minsk and Tartu, twice visited Tallinn, and then flew to Nice, all the while seeing, hearing, and smelling an empire fall to pieces and watching its inhabitants scramble for salvation from the collapsing debris. Few people could bear testimony to as much in their lifetimes, while I had seen time compressed, with decades becoming weeks and weeks becoming minutes. And now, for better or for worse, I was reentering this maelstrom that threatened to destroy us all rather than do the sensible thing, which was to go back home, have a pizza and beer, turn on the ball game, write my stories, and finally start my great American novel.

Pitun, like his supporters, imagined a frictionless comeback accompanied by the pealing of church bells and the adoring hallelujahs of his acolytes. That was surely quite possible. But no less possible was a scenario—*sic transit gloria mundi*, after all—that likely figured less prominently in his calculations: a chaotic and violent welcome spearheaded by the not insignificant numbers of his opponents, the thousands of political prisoners who would have been released in the chaos and the tens of thousands of ordinary citizens who had kept low profiles and remained hidden as silently as mice in their homes, avoiding encounters with the secret police, while sharpening their knives and honing their arguments for the day they would make their own triumphant return.

Civil war had already broken out in Russia, with Russians killing Russians, in addition to killing and being killed by non-Russians. I knew from Russian history that, when the *narod* succumbed to its most primitive, its basest instincts, as it periodically did in peasant and worker rebellions, the consequences for the country were always earth-shattering—and the spilt blood could fill entire reservoirs. And that was decidedly no exaggeration. Russian uprisings and civil wars resembled the ravages of swarms of locusts and hordes of Mongols. Even worse, they were like the plagues cast by a vengeful God on the ancient Egyptians. No one survived and the land would be ruined, a barren desert, for years to come.

Happy thoughts! Fortunately, both Pippa and I had no desire for conversation, so I was able to trudge through barren landscapes undisturbed, while she remained pensive and, for all I knew, equally committed to exploring the depths of despair. She caught me observing her and asked whether I wanted to go back to our suite. "No," I replied, "let's stay. I like looking out to sea. It's calming." She nodded and we resumed our separate conversations with our surroundings and ourselves.

But not for long. A distraught Lady Bird rushed into the dining car like a cyclone, one hand on her heaving bosom, the other covering her mouth. Her lipstick was smeared and her perfectly coiffed hair was un unsightly jumble of curls and strands. She stopped at our table, took several deep breaths, placed both hands together as if in prayer, and, clearly fighting hysteria and tears, cried, "Bobby Lee! It's Bobby Lee, Miss Pip-Puh! It's Bobby Lee, Mister Steven!"

"What's Bobby Lee?" Pippa enquired, her head cocked quizzically to the left.

"I've looked up and down the train and the boat and the poor dear"—she broke into tears—"and, and the poor dear is missing!"

"I'm sure he's somewhere," I said as calmly as I could. "Why don't all three of us go look for him, alright?"

Pippa had taken Lady Bird's hand and was stroking it. "I've got a better idea, Steven. You sit yourself down here, Miss Lady Bird, and Steven and I will scour the train and barge and I'm sure that a few minutes from now we'll be bringing the old rascal back to you. Why, I bet he's flirting with one of the waitresses or sleeping off a tad too much Bourbon."

Lady Bird fell into the chair and wearily sighed, "Oh, I do so hope y'all are right." With her chattering put to an abrupt halt by the unfolding tragedy, the poor girl was the picture of despair.

"We'll find that rascal," I insisted, "don't you worry, Lady Bird, we'll find him.

*

I was wrong: Bobby Lee was nowhere to be found. Pippa and I walked the length of the train thrice, knocking on every compartment, peering into bathrooms and closets, examining the pantry and refrigerators in the kitchen, looking through the luggage compartment in the last car. There was no Bobby Lee. Voronov, of course, had immediately enquired what we were up to and, as much as I didn't want to, we had to tell him—which proved to be for the better, as he mobilized several of his minions to help us with the search. When we had finished with the train, we began with the barge, effectively repeating the same procedure three times. But to no avail. Bobby Lee had vanished. In any case, he was nowhere on the barge or in the train.

Voronov then suggested that we speak to the crew of the barge. The captain and two of the crew had never caught sight of the big and colorful Texan. They would surely have remembered him, if they had seen him. The third crew member, however, a short man with a barrel chest and powerful arms who went by the name of Hanno Schmidt, thought he had glimpsed him on the bow of the barge early in the morning, just as the sun began to rise and the sea was rough and the deck was wet from the rain that had fallen in the night.

"Was he alone?" I wanted to know. Hannes nodded, but emphasized that he had his chores to do and saw the man for only a few seconds. As he had said, the American stood on the bow and his hands appeared to be on the railing and, as far as he could tell, he was looking out to sea. The sea could be magical, especially to people who rarely traveled by boat and he had seen many tourists stare out to sea, looking at nothing in particular, but presumably listening to the sorrowful sounds of the cawing gulls and contemplating the purpose of their lives. I wasn't expecting such an existential turn in the seaman's story, so I asked if Bobby Lee looked sad or depressed. Hannes raised his shoulders and shrugged. He couldn't tell. After all, *der Ami* was facing forward, while he was moving toward the stern and was occupied with his work.

"It's not impossible for the man to have slipped," the captain stated cautiously. "The deck was wet and some spots could have been slippery. Your friend was a big man—from Texas, yes?—who did not know boats and the sea and could easily have made a false step." His voice trailed off.

"And fallen into the sea?" Pippa hesitantly asked.

"*Es ist möglich*," the captain grunted. "It's possible. The space between the deck and the railing is big enough for even a big man to slip through." He pulled on his cigarette and produced a perfectly formed ring. "And if he fell into the water"—an unnecessary pause—"well, even a good swimmer would have had difficulty in such rough seas. Please excuse me for being so blunt, but I believe you should ask the Polish authorities if a body washed up on their shore."

"Let's search everything one more time," Pippa suggested. And we did, but with no more success than before. Bobby Lee was gone. It was, I told Pippa, possible that a man of his constitution might very well have survived. He might have made it to the shore or perhaps one of the many boats we had encountered had picked him up. Or Polish or Swedish fishermen.

"Or he's dead."

We broke the news and expressed our worst fears to Lady Bird—there was no use pretending that all would be well, we both agreed—but, instead of responding as we thought she would—by weeping hysterically and requiring immediate medical attention and possible sedation, Lady Bird leaned back thoughtfully in her chair, murmured, "So, it's come to this," excused herself, and, without thanking us for our efforts or expressing her grief, lumbered back to her compartment. Pippa and I were speechless. Her affection for Bobby Lee had appeared to be genuine; they had been in so many ways the perfect old couple that anticipated each other's moves and appreciated each other's company.

"She's one bloody strong lady," Pippa said. "I fully expected her to break down."

"So did I," I said. "She's a tough gal, she's a helluva tough gal. I wonder if—"

"—we've been underestimating her?"

"Wouldn't be the first time, would it?"

*

Later that day, before we sat down for lunch, Pitun informed the assembled crowd that his good and dear friend, Bobby Lee Houston, appeared to have had an unfortunate accident and slipped overboard. He spoke highly of his wisdom, goodness, courage, and desire to help Russia at its time of need. Bobby Lee would never be forgotten by the Russian people and he, Pitun, would make every effort to build a monument to this great hero in the city he loved so dearly—Moscow. Lady Bird stood tearfully by Pitun's side and, after he had finished, she added a few words of her own, ending with the promise that she would finish the great project that her beloved husband and partner for life had begun. She cast a gracious look at Pitun, who responded with a smile and a bow of his bald head. Odd, I thought. Odd that the otherwise irrepressible Lady Bird should not have spoken more concretely of what Bobby Lee had hoped to accomplish in Russia and just how Pitun fit in those plans. This was a perfect opportunity to endorse her boy and, instead, she gratified him only with a vague remark and a side glance. What was the old girl up to?

Before we dispersed to our tables, Voronov called for our attention and announced that we would be docking at Kaliningrad shortly after our repast. As it would take a few hours for the train to disembark and for supplies for the final leg of our journey to be procured, we were all welcome to take a stroll through this "ancient Russian" city—I heard Pippa snort when he said that—but, please, not to wander off too far, since our schedule was tight and getting tighter with every kilometer that we came nearer to St. Petersburg, founded by the great Tsar Peter as Russia's "fabled window to the West," which symbolized the "unbreakable bonds" between President Pitun and Europe. Voronov would have continued with his grandiloquence, I suspect, but Pitun tapped him on the wrist and he immediately stopped, ending with the curt wish that we take the president's words to heart and never forget the great Bobby Lee Houston.

"Balderdash!" Pippa exclaimed after we took our seats with our plates loaded down with blinis, sour cream, and caviar. "Those chaps couldn't give a farthing for Mister Houston. It was his money they were after and, judging from Lady Bird's Periclean oration, they're going to get it."

"Think so? I'm not so sure. The old girl's been acting strangely ever since Bobby Lee's vanishing act. The blinis, by the way, are superb." And then back on theme: "I wouldn't be surprised if she had something up her sleeve."

"Flabby arms, I should think," Pippa muttered in between chews. "You're right about the blinis." Then she stopped and looked plaintively at me. "Am I getting fat? I think I'm getting fat. Be honest, Steven. Am I getting fat?"

I knew enough about direct questions like that to know they should always be elided or evaded. "You're perfect," I gushed with all my Connecticut Yankee charm, "and you damned well know it, my dear." I caught Lady Bird looking in our direction and, impelled by a desperate desire to avoid potential pitfalls and certain embarrassment, I waved to her. She smiled in recognition, appeared to say something to Pitun and Voronov, and trundled off in our direction.

"How *are* you, dear, sweet Lady Bird?" Pippa asked after Lady Bird had piled on some blinis and occupied a chair. "You two were so, so close. It must be hard…"

Lady Bird took her hand and smiled. "As well as can be expected, dearie. Thanks much for asking. And"—turning to me—"you, too, Mister Steven. Thanks for looking up and down this tub for Bobby Lee. He loved you, Mister Steven—"

"And we loved him," I interjected.

"—and my husband wasn't no easy man to please. But he saw something in you, I think it was something that reminded him of himself. Well, y'all are still welcome to join the oil business. Ain't got much of a head for business and I'm shore we could use a man of your many talents. And"—now turning back to Pippa—"yours, too, dearie. Why, I dare say you'd love Texas. No, no—not immediately. But it grows on you and, after a while, you can't rightly tell that you've lived or wanted to live anywhere else."

"Would you like to join Steven and me for a walk in Kaliningrad?" Pippa asked quite unexpectedly. I admired her good heart, but had been hoping she and I wouldn't have to commiserate with or entertain anybody during the few minutes of free time Voronov had granted us.

"Oh, dearie," Lady Bird said with tears in her eyes, "you're one mighty fine lady, you are." And then, turning to me again: "And don't you forget it, Mister Steven, don't you ever forget it!"

CHAPTER SIX

Kaliningrad and St. Petersburg

Most of Kaliningrad was an irredeemably grim and monotonously Soviet city, typifying all that was least appealing about the uniquely drab drabness that Lenin's unimaginative heirs had invented and imposed on all the lands they had conquered. Except for a stretch of buildings along the waterfront, little of the former Königsberg appeared to have survived. On the positive side, many of the streets were lined with leafy trees, parks appeared to be amply provided, and the ornate domes of Orthodox churches and the simple spires of Protestant ones adorned the otherwise unimpressively flat skyline. Given that the city had been closed to the world in Soviet times and possessed a busy port, it was not quite as unattractive as I expected it to be—at least not in its entirety or the bit we could see near the wharf.

As we strolled along the bustling streets, I suddenly realized what I should have seen upon disembarking: there appeared to be no crisis, no collapse, no death and destruction here—which was all the more unusual in light of the news report a few days back of a joint Polish-Lithuanian attack on the province. Had the attackers been thrown back by the large numbers of Russian military and naval units stationed here? Or were enemy forces outside the city gates sharpening their knives and preparing for a final offensive? I could hear no shelling, but that could be deceptive. Meanwhile, the people we encountered appeared to be in no hurry to go anywhere. No signs of panic, no demonstrations, just sporadic sightings of armed soldiers.

"Well, at least Russia doesn't seem to be collapsing here," Pippa remarked.

"It shore ain't," Lady Bird seconded her.

"The calm before the storm?" I wondered. "They're shielded from Mother Russia by the Baltic states. It could take longer for the crisis to get here." My comment evoked no response, so I didn't pursue it. Besides, after Lady Bird grabbed hold of my arm and pressed my elbow against her side, all I could think of was the many folds of fat her dress concealed.

Pippa stopped, twirled her head from side to side, and pointed to a little café. "Coffee, anyone? I think we've seen all there is to see. Are your feet as tired as mine?"

"They shore are!"

The café, unoriginally called Café Kaliningrad, was lined with mirrors, a fake black marble floor, and ubiquitous brass railings, while the laminated tables came with exceptionally uncomfortable straight-back aluminum chairs. Our coffees arrived, served in tiny white plastic cups and with tiny colored plastic spoons. The waitress, a young girl with a broad face, blonde hair, ice-blue eyes, and strategically torn jeans, refused to smile, even after we thanked her effusively for the coffees.

"Here eez check," she informed us and carelessly dropped the receipt on the table. "Vater?"

"No, *nyet, spasibo*—thank you," I shook my head vigorously, doubting that Kaliningrad's water would be free of bacteria. The coffee had a rancid smell, but I took a sip anyway. The others had barely touched theirs as well. We would, I decided, be leaving soon.

"So, what's next for you, Miss Lady Bird?" Pippa quipped. "I mean in St. Petersburg and after?"

"I honestly don't know, dearie." Lady Bird took a sip and, frowning, pronounced, "Lord, this stuff ain't drinkable, is it? But to your question, sweetie, it's like this. This P'toon thing

—well, it was mostly Bobby Lee's project. He was the brains in the family, in case you hadn't noticed. I don't care much for politics—or business—whether here or in the US of A. Can't stand it, actually. Lots of old farts—pardon my French—arguing over nothing, as far as I can tell, rather than doing something useful with themselves. And this P'toon fella—well, I ain't shore he's any different from the rest of them coyotes. Now, Bobby Lee —Bobby Lee adored him and I shore as heck don't know why. I couldn't trust nobody with beady eyes—did you see them, dearie? No honest man has beady eyes, is what I say. But, heck, Bobby Lee would've wanted me to carry out his wishes, so I guess I'll just tag along until the show is over and then head for home." She smiled wistfully and turned from Pippa to me and back to Pippa again. "Texas! I shore do love that state. It's home and, as y'all know, there ain't no place like home, even if it ain't a castle."

I was only half-surprised by Lady Bird's observations (though I did notice that she appeared not to know that her husband's opinion of Pitun was equally low), so, in the spirit of openness, I decided to broach a topic that we had heretofore ignored. "Miss Lady Bird," I said, "I feel the same way about President Pitun. He's a little bald man with beady eyes and a greasy smirk. Reminds me of a bad used-car salesman." Lady Bird emitted a Texas-sized guffaw. "And the thing I've learned in my years as a journalist is that you need to trust your instincts and your first impressions. And Pitun, well, frankly, he's rubbed me the wrong way ever since we met him."

"The bastard's a creep," Pippa added matter-of-factly and then, speaking with greater ardor, proclaimed, "And I, for one, am *absolutely delighted* that your enthusiasm for him isn't quite what we thought it was."

"Oh, heaven forbid, sweetie," Lady Bird declared, "my daddy taught me how to recognize a sonofabitch a mile off and, when I saw that P'toon fella, I could smell a sonofabitch right off."

I resolved to push the envelope and, lowering my voice, asked, "Do you think it was an accident?"

"I would have," she replied, "but there's jes one thing that don't make no sense: my Bobby Lee was as agile and sure-footed as a mountain lion. Ain't no way he would've slipped."

I was going to ask the obvious follow-up question, but Lady Bird suddenly extended her hand and flashed her watch and cried, "Lord! It's getting late. Don't want to be stuck in this here shit hole, do we now? Oh, darn, pardon my French!"

On the way back to the train, we encountered a deeply unsettling sight: four long columns of marching, uniformed youths—both boys and girls—punching the air with their small fists and chanting "Pi-TUN! Pi-TUN! Pi-TUN!" Ominously, their uniforms were charcoal black with shiny brass buttons, black belts, and black leather boots. At the front of the columns, two youths brandished an outsized portrait of a severe-looking Pitun; others held Russian flags; still others carried signs, "Down with America," "Down with the Jews," "Down with Ukrainian Fascism."

We watched, mesmerized, horrified, and enervated, unable or too terrified to cut through their ranks and risk provoking some hothead. Pippa and Lady Bird grabbed my arms, in a futile attempt to draw strength from me. I held their hands so tightly that their knuckles turned white, but they showed no sign of discomfort. The scene before us neutralized whatever physical pain we might have felt. These boys and girls were no different from Hitler's Brown Shirts or Mussolini's Black Shirts. And it wasn't the hate they spewed that disturbed me; I had seen too much of that in my travels to ascribe too much importance to local manifestations of a global phenomenon. No, it was the dedication, the fervor, the fanaticism with which they obviously regarded Pitun. He was their leader, their *Führer*, their *vozhd*, their Messiah, and they looked like they'd be perfectly happy to sacrifice their lives at a moment's notice if only he commanded them to do so. Blind fanatics such as these could destroy the world in their vain hope to save Russia and its bald-headed, beady-eyed, megalomaniacal embodiment, Pitun.

Worse still, the huge crowd that watched them march was obviously supportive. Many cheered or whistled; others chanted along, punching the air with their angry fists. Still others held their right arms outstretched. Kaliningrad, I suddenly realized, may have looked unruffled on the outside, but, as was manifestly clear from this demonstration, passions were hot and blood was boiling on the inside. Pitun chose well in coming here.

And, as we discovered in a few minutes, the marchers hadn't assembled serendipitously. They stomped and screamed their way to the wharf with our train. Seeing the vast crowd of supporters, Pitun displayed his athletic agility by climbing atop one of the train cars and, turning to the wildly cheering masses, motioned to them to be quiet and then, with his smile metamorphosing into a fierce scowl, loudly proclaimed that he was coming back to Russia to save the Motherland from her enemies.

"Will we let the Americans make us slaves?" No, the audience shouted. "Will we sell our souls to the European pederasts and Jewish bankers?" No, they roared. "Will we permit Ukrainian and Estonian and other scum-like fascists take our democracy from us?" No!

He went on in this manner for a few minutes, mentioning every conceivable enemy and always eliciting the identical response. Then Pitun announced that he would soon, very soon, be in St. Petersburg, whence he would lead the brave Russian people against their dastardly enemies and to the final triumph of sacred, holy, eternal Mother Russia.

"Are you with me? Will you march with me? Will you take up arms and save Mother Russia?" he screamed, his neck bulging, his face as red as borscht, his hands waving. *"Da! Da! Da!"*

At that moment, the train whistle blew, Pitun bowed, smiled, and blew kisses to the marchers, and, nimbly making his way down—for a moment I caught myself hoping that he would fall and either elicit laughter or break his thick neck—waved to his adoring fans, and disappeared into one of the cars.

We quickly followed, but not before a blonde girl of about eighteen, who could easily have passed for a prime specimen of the Aryan race, focused her rabid gaze on us and shouted, "*Zhidi!* Jews! Go home to America!" None of us felt impelled to correct her misperception, which may have angered her even more, for, as we rushed to board the train, she cast a Coca-Cola can and struck poor Lady Bird, who, like Lot's unfortunate spouse, had looked back for one last glimpse of the crowd, in the forehead.

"It's nothing," she said, as Pippa took her flustered face in her hands. "Jes a little cut." And then she resumed her usual jocular pose: "Why, back home they would've thrown rocks. If this is the best these folks can do, heck, they ain't never gonna win."

"Let's hope so," I said lamely, disconcerted by the marchers, their slogans, and, most of all, by Pitun, who had finally shown his true colors. This was no longer the dapper gentleman we had stumbled upon in the Negresco. This was the vicious, bloody dictator and manipulator who had ruled Russia for so many decades. This was the real Pitun—and Pippa and I were his unwilling cheerleaders. I had argued consistently against doing anything to stop him, much to Pippa's frustration. These events had pushed my views in the contrary direction. I decided we should do something. But what?

*

Once inside the train, we headed for Lady Bird's compartment, where Pippa ordered her to lay her huge frame on the bed and applied a cold compress to her forehead. Lady Bird, unsurprisingly, tolerated such solicitude for no more than a few minutes and, gently placing Pippa's hand on the bed, shook her head and sat upright. Then she announced, "That was jes dreadful," and looked searchingly at us. I squirmed a bit, suddenly less sure of my resolve, but finally blurted, "We should do something!" Pippa cast an uncomprehending look in my direction. "I know, Pippa, I know. But now, after what we just saw—after what they called us and tried to do to us—"

"They would have killed us, you know," Pippa pointed out.

"—well, now I feel differently. I think we should try."

"It's my turn to be devil's advocate," she replied. "Very well, Steven, let's do something." And then, after a suspenseful interval: "Exactly, *what*?" I said nothing and she resumed her train of thought. "And there, ladies and gentlemen, is the rub. What can two correspondents with compromised reputations and a widow from Texas do against a man with adoring millions, purloined billions, and a few dozen nuclear warheads? Or is the question too rhetorical?"

This indecisive back and forth went on for a while, with Pippa prodding, me responding with generalities and vague hopes. It was obvious that neither of us had a clue as to what could or should be done. We were pen-pushers who lived in the world of texts and made irregular expeditionary forays into the real world of real people, whom we did not really know and whose political behavior we observed with skill, but could not comprehend or replicate. We were blustering tyros, cheap amateurs, wannabe experts who knew nothing of real politics, which involved guns and bombs and blackmail and mendacity and all the things that made us uncomfortable. "Do what?" I had once asked and, now, Pippa had, too. Pitun would know. Rougement would know. Even the two Russians from the Union of Patriots could give a half-baked answer to this question. In contrast, we were able only to dance around it, too terrified to take it in our arms and execute a waltz. I listened glumly to Pippa's despairing lecture on our impotence, when Lady Bird quietly enquired, "May I say something, y'all?"

We had almost forgotten that she was the third party to our dialogue. Pippa stopped talking and, smiling endearingly at the poor thing, said, "Of course. As you can see, this is going nowhere, so if you have any ideas for getting out of this *cul de sac*, by all means let's hear them."

"Cool de what, dearie?" Lady Bird actually fluttered her eyelashes as she spoke.

"Dead end," Pippa replied drily.

"Right. Okay. Well," she began, "let me tell y'all what we rascals once did in high school to our least favorite teacher, Mister Tunny. He taught math and we all hated him. A tough grader and, as Bobby Lee would say, a real sonofabitch. Pardon the French," she said cheerfully. "Well, we all wanted to get back at Mister Tunny, as y'all can well imagine. But how, right? What can a bunch of kids do to a teacher that would really, and I mean *really*, teach him a lesson he'd never forget? Pretty much nothing, right? We were in one of them cool de sacks, too, until one day—it was a week or so before graduation—one of the kids, a pimply boy that everyone always made fun of cause he was a genius at science—I jes remembered his name was Homer! yep, it was Homer Vergil Thrace, if you can believe it—well, this pimply boy named Homer Vergil Thrace—a funny name, ain't it?—said he'd read about this drug, a special kind of laxative, that gave you the runs. What we in Texas call Montezuma's RE-venge. And depending on how much of the stuff a person ingested, you could more or less determine the exact time of the, well, runs. So, where do we get our hands on the stuff? We all cried. And Homer Vergil Thrace smiled that pimply smile of his and said he could make the stuff in the chem lab. Well, shore enough, he did and one of us girls managed to slip it into Mister Tunny's coffee just before the graduation ceremony during which he was supposed to give the gala address to the assembled guests and parents. And, shore enough, jes as that boy Homer said, right in the middle of his speech we heard this in-cre-di-ble rumble and—"

Pippa held her hand over her mouth and couldn't restrain her giggles. "Okay, okay, we get it. No need to go into details." When her laughter subsided, Lady Bird finally posed the question that both of us dreaded: "You in on this, Steven?" I nodded. "Dearie?" Pippa had no choice but to express her agreement as well. Then, one of us posed the obvious question: "So, where do get the stuff?"

Lady Bird adopted an aw-shucks look and replied, "Why, as luck would have it, Bobby Lee always carried it with him. Y'all know, his digestion didn't always, well, y'all know..."

"Then we're in business!" Pippa cried and kissed Lady Bird and me. And with that, the three of us became co-conspirators in what we called Operation Montezuma.

*

We lurched backward and, with the steward announcing that we would be in St. Petersburg in the morning, the train resumed its waltz-like beat and, after winding carefully through coils of tracks, left Kaliningrad behind and, with its speed increasing until the houses and trees became blurs, headed northeast for the final act of our madcap adventure.

We had blithely and overenthusiastically agreed to Lady Bird's crazy plan, but, now that I had a few minutes to consider it without passion and anger, I quickly stumbled upon the all-too-obvious fact that it was the height of insanity, not because it wouldn't destroy Pitun, but because we'd never pull it off. The first obstacle was slipping the chemical into Pitun's drink, be it coffee, tea, or something stronger. Just how was that to be done—and by whom? By the gargantuan Lady Bird, who attracted attention to herself simply by breathing and heaving her enormous bosom? By the diminutive Pippa who had never in her life engaged in such a preposterous escapade? Or by me, an overprivileged and overeducated brat with no knowledge of the real world?

Then there was the question of amount and timing.

Assuming we could overcome the first obstacle, we immediately ran up against the second. If we applied too little of the chemical or did so too late, its effect would kick in only after Pitun's encounter with his adoring followers. If, alternatively, too much or too early, then he'd suffer the consequences before leaving the train. Neither Lady Bird nor Pippa nor I had the medical training to make the determination. At best, we'd have to rely on guesswork and hope for luck.

Finally, and not least consequential, should we succeed, should Pitun be embarrassed, his entourage and his followers would immediately start the search for the guilty party or parties. Most of the people on the train were Russian or Pitun's declared supporters and, hence, above immediate suspicion. At whom, then, would accusatory fingers be pointed? Obviously, at the stewards and waiters, and at the foreigners—that is to say, at us. Lady Bird, as the grieving widow of the heroic philanthropist Bobby Lee, might get a break, but the two interlopers and certified sneaks—one of whom had family ties to a slew of American spy agencies—would become the prime suspects.

Naturally, they might, after interrogating us, set us free. Or they might not. And if General Fedotov and his lunatic fringe got involved in the investigation, then chances were that we'd be arrested, whereupon all bets would be off. Russia was in chaos, fighting and bloodshed were everywhere, and no one would miss, or care about the sad fate of, two errant journalists who bit off more than they could chew. During the Civil War of 1918-1921, the Bolshevik Cheka showed no restraint whatsoever, gleefully killing presumed enemies of the people if they deemed it necessary and expeditious to do so. Smooth hands were a dead giveaway of bourgeois, priestly, or intellectual backgrounds and virtually guaranteed a bullet in the skull. I wouldn't be surprised if Fedotov and his boys applied similar measures to determine the degree of one's loyalty to Pitun. There would almost surely be torture as well. We would sing at the very sight of Fedotov's scalpels and pliers and execution would immediately follow.

In sum, our prospects of success were close to nil, while our prospects of meeting a most unhappy end were close to certain. A hulking factory, red from rust and, possibly, embarrassment at its Soviet origins, distracted me for a few seconds, but, as soon as the bucolic countryside reappeared, my thoughts assumed a decidedly somber quality once again. I would, I decided, have to persuade Pippa and Lady Bird that the plan had to be abandoned. Pippa, I suspected, could probably be convinced: she was more level-headed than me and had, as far as I could tell, not a whit of good old-fashioned heroism lurking in the deepest recesses of her soul. Lady Bird would be a tougher nut to crack, partly because she was distraught by Bobby Lee's disappearance and might want to lash out at somebody, anybody, and mostly because she was a loose cannon by nature. Convincing Pippa alone wouldn't alleviate our predicament, because merely knowing of Lady Bird's intentions—however much we might plead that we opposed them—made us accomplices, possibly in a real court of law and definitely in Fedotov's court of lawlessness. In effect, all three of us were bound by the stupid vagaries of fate that had propelled us all to make an absurdly suicidal decision. We were in it together or out of it together. There was, alas, no halfway solution.

Lady Bird was asleep, while Pippa was reading some magazine. I tapped her knee, placed a finger on my lips, and sidled up to her, whispering, "I've been thinking. This scheme is crazy." Pippa nodded in agreement. "It'll get us all killed." I looked at her quizzically and, nodding again, she returned my whisper: "I agree. But now we've got to convince *her* and that won't be easy. Give me a drink."

I knocked the bottle against the glass and Lady Bird's eyes opened. She cleared her throat and smiled, removing an errant lock of hair from her wrinkled forehead. "Sorry about that," she growled, "I jes couldn't resist that sleeping bug." She peered through the window. "I see we left that dreadful Kalingrad. How long was I out?"

"Maybe half an hour," I replied. "By the way, Pippa and I have been thinking…"

"Y'all want to bail, right? Y'all figure our plan won't work or we'll get into trouble, right?"

"Well, yes," I stammered, embarrassed by the transparency of our unease. But if we couldn't hide our feelings from Lady Bird, how likely were we to be able to conceal our plans from Pitun and friends?

"Don't y'all worry," she said confidently. "I've got it all figured out." And then Lady Bird proceeded with what sounded like a prepared lecture on the ease of using this particular chemical to produce embarrassing consequences. "It really is a piece of cake," she opined, "believe you me. And don't you worry, Miss Pip-Puh: I'll handle everything and slipping that stuff will be a piece of cake for you. P'toon likes you. He'll be looking at your face and tits—pardon the French—and not at his drink." The skepticism had obviously not faded from our faces, for she then resumed with her upbeat explanation. "And if y'all are worried about the aftermath, don't be. Me and Bobby Lee have a good friend in Saint Pete"—I wondered if she knew we were traveling to Russia and not to northern Florida—"who'll get us out of the city and the country faster than you can say the Alamo."

"An American? A Russian?"

"One of us, of course. Let's jes say he's well connected." Her face was glowing from the enthusiasm and determination with which she spoke. This was a Lady Bird that I hadn't seen before. The flighty airhead appeared to have become a resolute fighter for world peace and justice. Quite probably she had always had that side to her, but Bobby Lee's domineering behavior hadn't let it come to the fore—until now. With him gone, Lady Bird could be on the outside the person she had always been on the inside. It took considerable forbearance, self-discipline, and self-restraint to play the role of a poor second fiddle for so long. This Texan lady was clearly no nincompoop. Although Operation Montezuma still struck me as a hare-brained scheme worthy of Khrushchev in his wildest moments, the self-assurance with which she defended and explained it filled me with renewed confidence. The thought of being in Lady Bird's muscular hands had terrified me a few minutes ago; now, that same thought had magically become a source of comfort. I could see from the changing expressions on Pippa's face that she had undergone a similar transformation.

"So, are y'all in?" Lady Bird cried. "All for one and one for all?"

"Very well," Pippa said with some lingering hesitation.

"We must be crazy, but okay."

"Y'all won't regret it," Lady Bird assured us. "And y'all will never forget what you did. I do say I think our countries will be proud of us—and maybe the Russians, too. Drink on it? Bourbon for me, sweetie."

We elevated our glasses and, as the sunlight struck the crystal and broke up into its constituent colors, I couldn't help thinking that the image could be interpreted either as reflecting the beauty of our plan or the likelihood that it would fall apart. Well, we were in, as Lady Bird said, so that additional misgivings were now to be avoided at all cost. And if worse came to worst, well, there was always the prospect of laudatory obits in all the newspapers of the world. Life was preferable to being remembered kindly, but so be it.

*

We spent the next few hours going over our plan, if that's what our fantastic improvisations could be called. Two things, said Lady Bird, required our immediate attention. The first was obvious: how would Pippa slip the chemical into Pitun's food or drink? We quickly agreed that adding it to his food would be impractical. That meant getting the damned stuff into his drink.

Lady Bird suggested that since we'd be arriving in St. Petersburg in the morning, Pippa would have the opportunity during breakfast.

"Would Pitun eat breakfast on the eve of such a momentous day?" I wondered.

"Of course," Lady Bird dismissed my doubts with a resolute wave of the hand. "We know he always has breakfast and we also know he always has the same thing for breakfast—three eggs, scrambled, buttered toast, a side of pickled herring, and a pot of very black coffee." Who exactly was *we* and how did they know such details? I wanted to ask, but didn't, assuming she meant Bobby Lee and herself.

"After he starts," Lady Bird went on with her battle plan, "y'all will have to join him and—"

"Won't he consider us a rude interruption?" It was Pippa's turn to be rebuked.

"Not at all, sweetie," Lady Bird answered with a trace of condescension. "He'll expect y'all to talk with him about his coming victory. After all, y'all are the official chroniclers, ain't you? So, y'all wouldn't be doing your job if y'all failed to meet him, right?

"And then"—and she bored her eyes into mine—"this is most important, Mister Steven. Y'all listening? You'll have to seat yourself opposite P'toon and keep him distracted with your questions and praise, while you, Miss Pip-Puh, you'll be sitting next to him, real close-like, and, when he's delivering one of his orations—y'all have noticed that the fella shore likes to talk like a preacher—y'all will extend your hand to get something —"

"What?"

"Don't matter, dearie. Salt, sugar, bread—whatever happens to be within reach and near his coffee cup. Right, dearie?" Lady Bird fluttered her eyelashes, though I could sense she was getting annoyed with our amateurishness. "So, as I was saying, you'll extend your hand and, while it's floating over P'toon's coffee, you drop one of these tiny little pills"—and she showed us one—"and that's that." She smiled broadly, proud of having successfully explained so simple a task to two developmentally challenged children.

"You make it sound so easy," Pippa muttered uncertainly. "What if he catches me?"

"Well, for starters, dearie, he won't—unless you mess it up. And if you do, jes remember that it's curtains for all of us." Lady Bird laughed loudly, presumably to mitigate the impact of what she had just told us. "So, you'll be extra-careful, won't you, dearie?" Where did this commandeering tone, this poise, this self-assurance come from? Bobby Lee's untimely expiration must have unleashed a hidden demon in his spouse's soul.

"Anyway," and she held up the pill again, "it's jes a teeny-weeny tiny, little pill. Lord, it won't even make a plopping sound when it falls into the coffee. And it dissolves pretty much instantly." And then a cautionary tone. "Jes make shore he drinks it, right, dearie? But you're a clever girl, ain't you? So, I'm shore you'll think of something. Ain't that right?"

And Pippa, in a school girl's tone: "I guess so."

Fully in command, Lady Bird directed her gaze at each of us and, adopting a deathly serious voice, added: "Oh, and there's one more thing. I'll join y'all after a few minutes, jes to make shore everything's A-okay and to persuade that nice Mister P'toon that he jes *must* wear his white uniform that day. Y'all understand why, right?"

We nodded in assent. Pippa, I noticed, had turned quite red.

"And you think this'll work?" I desperately wanted reassuring.

"Piece of cake!" Lady Bird cried. "P'toon's a leader and

a man, sweetie." Her tone had become slightly condescending again. "Leaders and men love attention and flattery, don't they, Mister Steven?" I remained mum, knowing there was no way I could possibly answer that question without unleashing a storm of anger from at least one of the two women. "So, while you, Mister Steven, will be appealing to his political ego and encouraging him to imagine all the glory days ahead, you, Miss Pip-Puh, will be appealing to his male ego by flapping your eyelashes, touching his hand and arm real nice-like, and maybe even letting your leg bump into his, accident-like, of course."

"You expect *me* to flirt with that—that *monster*?"

"Y'all journalists do that all the time, don't you, dearie?" Lady Bird assumed a tone of mock innocence, as if she had never encountered self-serving, mendacious, and corrupt behavior in all her life. "You know exactly what I mean, don't you, Miss Pip-Puh? A little bit of bump and grind, a little bit of wiggling, maybe a tear or two out of those pretty little eyes of yours and you can have any politician, any cop, any *man* eating out of the palm of your hand." Then, turning to me: "Sorry, Mister Steven, but your sex is pretty pitiful, if you ask me." Back to Pippa: "So, shore, dearie, I don't think you'll have any trouble twisting that P'toon fella around your little finger and dropping that teeny-weeny pill into his coffee cup."

Lady Bird was right, of course. Pippa, despite her infrequent adoption of girlish mannerisms, was one of the toughest journalists I knew. She wouldn't have gotten as far as she did, had she not been capable of surviving the most extreme conditions and the most obnoxious individuals in pursuit of a lead. And I, for one, knew for a fact that she never hesitated to employ her feminine wiles, even when such behavior transparently contradicted her feminist beliefs and appeared to reinforce stereotypes of women as helpless and voiceless hysterics.

Frankly, I was far more worried about myself than about Pippa. What Lady Bird failed to mention was that, as this charade was taking place, I would have to maintain my cool and pretend not to notice what Pippa was doing. I'd have to play the role of the single-minded correspondent who was utterly, blindly, and completely focused on his job. Obviously, I, too, had been around the block numerous times; and, as Bobby Lee said, this wasn't my first rodeo. I'd stayed focused many times in the past; I'd played roles and exuded a false sincerity even more often. That was all part of the job and, if you didn't know that when you started out, you quickly learned it. You had to if you wanted to survive the cut-throat competition. But never to my recollection had I had to play such a role when the stakes —our lives and Russia's survival—were so high. Heroism wasn't my métier. I knew I could play the hero—and the villain—but I strongly doubted that I could *be* a hero. That took guts, which I had, but only in distinctly limited amounts.

This Lady Bird Houston, on the other hand, had guts galore. Bobby Lee's disappearance and likely death (at Pitun's hand?) hadn't just unleashed a demon; it had also revealed a vengeful streak that I had until now never noticed. The perfect, and perfectly charming and polite, Southern belle, Lady Bird, had demonstrated in the last few days that she also possessed a vengeful side that would have made her the pride of Sicilian mobsters pursuing a vendetta. From the moment that we expressed our initial, somewhat hesitant, agreement to the plan, Lady Bird had taken full control and transformed us, two of the world's top reporters, into her factotums. We had become putty in her fingers. She had a convincing retort to every objection; she exuded optimism and self-confidence; and she, unlike us, actually seemed to know what she was doing. How could we resist her talismanic powers? Obviously, we couldn't.

As Pippa and I learned at breakfast the next day, neither could Pitun. We followed Lady Bird's instructions to the letter. Pitun was delighted to see us and motioned to us to join him. I plied him with questions and scribbled incessantly in my notebook, while Pippa smiled and batted her eyelashes and even purred. Then, as he was heatedly laying out his plans for Russia's glorious future, I witnessed her lily-white hand float over the table, hesitate for a millisecond over his coffee, and then alight on the bread basket, whence she removed a croissant. Lady Bird then appeared, almost as if by magic, and, playing her role of the star-struck Texan millionairess perfectly, spoke adoringly of how handsome he looked in white and wouldn't he want to wear that lovely white uniform when he skips off the train in St. Petersburg? Pitun didn't hesitate for a second. He nodded vigorously, said it was an excellent idea, and then excused himself.

Lady Bird sat back and grinned. "What did I tell y'all? Like shooting fish in a barrel."

Both Pippa and I, however, were exhausted by the proceedings and, when Lady Bird suggested we go to her compartment for a "quick one" before we got ready to disembark, we nodded in unison and, holding hands (hers, I noticed, was as sweaty as mine), followed Lady Bird's elephantine waddle for the last time on this fateful train.

*

Reducing its speed, the train slowly pulled into St. Petersburg's Vitebsk Station, a glorious Art Nouveau structure erected before World War I. Too bad, I thought: it would have been nice to travel "to the Finland Station," the title of Edmund Wilson's famous book about Lenin's fateful arrival in Russia in the spring of 1917. That would have been more symbolically appropriate for what Pitun had in mind, but getting there would have required taking a variety of circuitous routes and he probably decided to forego the symbolism and save time.

The platform and station were packed with thousands of Pitun's supporters, shouting, chanting, waving Russian flags, bearing all manner of religious and imperialist signs. They were young and old, men and women, civilians and soldiers. I watched their faces as we came to a stop. They emanated a savage mixture of hope, despair, anger, and lunacy. These people were awaiting their Savior, the man who would restore stability and greatness to Russia and prosperity and comfort to them. They differed in no respect from the columns of marching Black Shirts we had encountered in Kaliningrad. These people would, I felt certain, kill, smash, and destroy anybody or anything that fell afoul of their leader's convictions or tastes. We three—the intrepid Lady Bird, the clever Pippa, and the fearful Steven—were entering the maws of this untamed and dangerous beast and, even if we pulled off our trick, who knew if we could possibly escape the mob's passions.

"This is perfect, jes perfect," Lady Bird observed. "Bet y'all a dollar that our boy P'toon decides to climb onto the car and repeat his Kalingrad performance. He has to greet the crowd and he can't very well do it with all those people pressing in on him from all sides." Her eyes assumed a malicious look. "And once he's up there, there ain't no place to hide, right? So, when the explosion comes—and it shore will, cause you and I know that the fella loves to hear his own voice—it's gonna come with a big bang." Uncontrollable giggles and a half-hearted attempt to cover her mouth followed.

Lady Bird's insouciance alarmed me. Yes, I was grateful for the confidence she conveyed, a quality that was in dwindling supply in me, especially as the prospect of being torn to pieces by these animals became all too real. But escaping the station could be a tricky proposition. A frenzied mob might decide to make an example of what awaits Russia's enemies by pummeling us to death. None of us looked Russian: our clothes, our haircuts, our shoes immediately gave us away. And my Russian, however proficient, was accented and would be recognized as such by any native with hearing.

A cheer swept through the crowd and, a few seconds later, we could hear Pitun's voice magnified with a bullhorn. Lady Bird slammed the window open and, leaning out with her massive torso and wiggling her imposing behind, crooked her head and reported that she could see a bit of "the fella." He was, she announced gleefully, dressed in an immaculate white uniform that he reserved only for special occasions. Then, as he spoke, at first with deliberate slowness and then with growing speed and violence, she translated his comments, intermittently adding her own interjections, such as bravo, good show, and the like. Pippa and I exchanged skittish glances and occasional nods that signified nothing other than a recognition of the other person's presence. "How will we get out of here?" I whispered. Pippa shrugged and raised her eyebrows.

Lady Bird's frame emerged from the window and, wiping her brow, she exclaimed, "That fella shore can talk! I bet he'll be up there for another thirty minutes, maybe more. Which means—oh, you poor things! Why, you're trembling, ain't y'all? —which means we can start our getaway."

"How can we get out? The station is packed wall-to-wall."

"Don't you worry your pretty little head, Mister Steven, I've got it all figured out. We'll go to the back of the train and make a nice little exit from the caboose. Then we'll cross the tracks and leave by one of the side doors, where there ain't gonna be that much folk milling about." She looked at us proudly, as if she had just revealed a state secret.

"And then what?" I enquired gloomily. "We'll still be stuck in this place."

"Maybe not, Mister Steven," she grinned mysteriously. "Jes trust me, alright?"

We took our things and, with the surprisingly agile Lady Bird leading the way—I noticed that she carried only a bulging handbag—made for the caboose. As she had predicted, there were no crowds in the back and we were able to hop off and cross over to the adjacent platform. Pippa and I traversed the rails gingerly, almost as if we feared touching a deadly third rail, while Lady Bird defied her size and bulk and simply glided across them, as if she negotiated rails every day. Some twenty yards away was an unguarded exit and, just as I was about to make a dash for it and freedom, Lady Bird grabbed my shoulder and said we should first have a coffee at the little bistro, relax a bit, and watch the show.

"Are you insane?" I muttered. "Let's get out of here as soon as—"

"Trust me, Mister Steven," she glanced at her watch and, hoping to settle our nerves, said, "Jes relax. I've got everything under control."

I was livid, but Pippa, who seemed to have succumbed completely to Lady Bird's iron will, said nothing, so, seething with anger and fearful of, well, death, I acceded to Missus Houston's wishes and helplessly watched her order three coffees.

"Sugar?" she enquired sweetly. "I always take four."

There was a sudden brief pause in Pitun's peroration. He stopped speaking for just under a second and one wouldn't have been remiss in thinking he did that for rhetorical effect, but Lady Bird nodded sagely and informed us that the "show would commence any second now." Then, finishing her coffee and smacking her lips, she ordered us to finish up and "skedaddle." Our job was done and it was time—finally! I wanted to say—to make our escape.

"Our cell phones!" Pippa cried. "We forgot to take them back."

"Don't you worry your pretty little head over that, dearie. I'll buy y'all new ones when we're outta here."

Outside, Lady Bird motioned to a sleek, black Volga and, as it slid up to the curb, Pippa and I followed Lady Bird inside, where we came upon the darkened silhouette of a large man in a bowler hat, holding an umbrella in both hands and humming "The International." I wanted to reverse my steps and remind Lady Bird that the taxi was taken, when a loud voice boomed, "Howdy, Steven!" It was, of all people, Bobby Lee. Before I could say anything, the door slammed shut, the motor roared to life, and we made our getaway.

*

"You're probably wondering." Lady Bird, openly giggling, spoke in perfectly articulated Queen's English. Needless to say, Pippa and I were speechless.

"It's all quite simple, old boy." Now it was Bobby Lee's turn to surprise us with an upper-class British accent. "We work for Her Majesty. Can't tell you more than that, I'm afraid, but I suppose you know how to connect the dots."

"And the bit about the CIA and the oil business?" I had regained my voice.

"Oh, just pulling your leg and having a spot of fun."

"So, you've been planning this all along?"

"Not quite," Lady Bird said. "We were planning something a tad less pacific, actually, but then we came upon you two and Bobby Lee—"

"Not his real name, I suppose," I grumbled.

"Quite. Neither is Lady Bird, of course. In any case, when we saw how lovely you two were, we decided to make the best of the opportunity which presented itself and resort to more civilized means. Besides, why make a martyr of the chap when you can humiliate him? More effective, don't you think?"

"And devilishly clever, too," Lady Bird said. "Don't you agree?"

"So, we were chumps, your patsies."

"Well, Mister Steven, that's one way of looking at it," Bobby Lee replied. "We'd prefer to say you were a jolly good fellow and helped Her Majesty—oh, and the free world."

"So, you obviously staged your disappearance," Pippa said.

"Had to, my dear, when it became evident that we were going to Kaliningrad. Change of plans necessitated a change of plans."

"And the computers?"

"My idea," Bobby Lee said with feigned humility. "Increased their uncertainty level, like my disappearance. Made then worry about you two, put them off guard. Oh," he chuckled, "I should say that it also threw you off balance. Made you a tad more susceptible to, er, Lady Bird's blandishments. A nice touch, actually, don't you think?"

"But," Lady Bird confessed, "I do think we went a mite overboard with those sleeping pills."

"Quite," Bobby Lee opined. "Quite unnecessary in retrospect. On the other hand," he grinned maliciously, "they did unnerve you. And that was the point."

"Why didn't you tell us who you were and what you were up to?" I demanded angrily. "You should have, you know."

"Couldn't do that, old boy. For one thing, we had to make sure you weren't the great man's fellow travelers. You must admit that your exalted status could have easily been interpreted as signifying ideological infatuation. For another, you might not have agreed to help the cause." He looked me in the eyes. "Would you?" I said nothing. "Precisely, old boy, precisely." And then, after he winked, came the touché: "Oh, and you may want to do something about your inordinate fancy for demon rum." I was going to respond with a *tu quoque* and say something about glass houses and stones, but decided to stay mum.

"All's well that ends well, right?" Lady Bird added. "No hard feelings? You'll be home soon and can still write the definitive Pitun tale. But"—and Lady Bird placed a finger on her lips —"you may not write about us, I'm afraid."

"Not even as Mister and Missus James Bond?" I said with

unconcealed sarcasm.

"Would be a serious breach," Bobby Lee admonished me. "London would frown. So would Washington—and Langley. Maybe even more than frown."

I looked at Pippa and saw that she was unsuccessfully repressing an onslaught of giggles. "Steven, you really must admit that this is hilarious." I gave her a dark stare. "Oh, don't look so angry. What's there to be angry about? We thought we were using *them*, but all this while they were using *us*! And you must admit that their accents and getups were brilliant. Never for a moment did I suspect—"

"You once said," I had a sudden epiphany and spoke directly to Lady Bird, "that *we* know what Pitun had for breakfast."

She reddened. "A slip of the tongue, I'm afraid. I had to think quickly and the excitement of the moment got the better of me, alas."

"And your sudden transformation from a Southern belle to a calm, cool, and collected manipulator?"

"Had to, of course. Was it that obvious?"

"And," recalling her excellent translation of Pitun's rooftop speech a few minutes ago, I resumed my interrogation, "you speak perfect Russian."

"*Konechno*," she said without a trace of an accent, "of course."

"*Ya tozhe*," added Bobby Lee. "Me, too."

Wide-eyed, though not as surprised as I should have been, I joined in Pippa's laughter. "What happens now? Or are we stuck in this dank place forever?"

"The train for Helsinki departs in thirty minutes," Bobby Lee informed us. At that moment, we heard a distant roar coming from the direction of the station.

"I do believe Señor Montezuma has just had his revenge,"

Lady Bird stated drily. "Indeed, we may have witnessed Pitun's last stand."

"The chemical?" I asked stupidly. What else could she have been talking about?

"Worked like a charm," Bobby Lee nodded. "Always does. British product, by the way. Rule Britannia and all that, I dare say." Then, while stroking Lady Bird's hand, he added, "Kudos to you, my dear. Brava, bravissima! A performance worthy of a prima donna." As a denouement, he brushed his lips against Lady Bird's hand. Whatever remained of my ill humor vanished: Russia might have fallen, but civilization, though weakened and possibly fatally wounded, was still alive. *Vita brevis, ars longa.*

"Good heavens," Pippa, flushed with the realization of what had just happened to Pitun, exclaimed, "I almost pity the poor man."

"Consider the far more sanguinary alternative which Lady Bird convinced me to abandon before I jumped ship," Bobby Lee reminded her. "So, all's well that ends well." Turning to Lady Bird, "You were about to say, dearest?"

"Thank you, my dear," she said. "I was going to say that we thought you two would appreciate the historical symmetry. Back to you, my love."

"Mister Pitun, whose travails are probably over by now, hoped to follow in Lenin's footsteps," he continued. "And," Lady Bird went on, "Bobby Lee and I thought both of you, being exceptionally literary types, would appreciate doing the reverse and depart from—" She paused, her broad face adorned with a malicious smirk. "Can you guess?"

Pippa and I saw the light at the same time and, like overeager schoolchildren currying the teacher's favor, cried, "*from the Finland Station!*"

END

ABOUT THE AUTHOR

Alexander J. Motyl

Alexander J. Motyl (b. 1953, New York) is a writer, painter, and professor. Nominated for the Pushcart Prize in 2008 and 2013, he is the author of nine novels, Whiskey Priest, Who Killed Andrei Warhol, Flippancy, The Jew Who Was Ukrainian, My Orchidia, Sweet Snow, Fall River, Vovochka, and Ardor; of two collections of poetry, Vanishing Points and Worries; and of a memoir, Bits and Pieces. His artwork has been shown in solo and group shows in New York, Philadelphia, Westport, and Toronto and is part of the permanent collections of the Ukrainian Museum in New York and the Ukrainian Cultural Centre in Winnipeg. He teaches political science at Rutgers University-Newark and is the author of seven academic books and numerous articles. According to Academic Influence, Motyl was ranked sixth among the "Top Ten Most Influential Political Scientists Today."